Homestead

A. K. Frailey

ISBN: 978-1-7323952-7-5

Website
https://akfrailey.com/

Amazon Author Page
https://www.amazon.com/A.-K.-Frailey/e/B006WQTQCE

The Writings of A. K. Frailey

Books for the Mind and Spirit

https://akfrailey.com/

Contact

akfrailey@yahoo.com

Historical Science Fiction Novels

OldEarth ARAM Encounter

OldEarth Ishtar Encounter

OldEarth Neb Encounter

OldEarth Georgios Encounter

OldEarth Melchior Encounter

Science Fiction Novels

Homestead

Last of Her Kind

Newearth Justine Awakens

Newearth A Hero's Crime

Short Stories

It Might Have Been—
And Other Short Stories 2nd Edition

One Day at a Time and Other Stories

Encounter Science Fiction
Short Stories & Novella 2nd Edition

Inspirational Non-Fiction

My Road Goes Ever On—Spiritual Being, Human Journey 2nd Edition

My Road Goes Ever On—A Timeless Journey

The Road Goes Ever On—A Christian Journey Through The Lord of the Rings

Children's Book

The Adventures of Tally-Ho

Poetry

Hope's Embrace & Other Poems 2nd Edition

Audible Versions Now Available.
Check book details on Amazon
for current listings.

Chapter One

No Place I'd Rather Be

My world ended on a Thursday.

It should have been a normal day. Well, as normal as seeing my daughter, Dana, off to her new life in St. Louis could be. I stood on the driveway, my stomach churning with the impending loss, and watched the last preparations finalized.

The bright sky was alive with sparrows, robins, blue jays, and a couple of cardinals fluttering about in springtime joy. The field across the road had greened up with winter wheat while the plowed fields down the road waited in lumpy hillocks to be planted. Redbuds swelled on the treetops populating the edge of our property. With a lungful of sweet air, I tried to calm my jittery nerves. *She'll be okay.*

Dana's car, stuffed with two kitchen chairs, bedding, the last of her clothing, enough comfort food to get her through the first week, and a miraculous medal and prayerbook she didn't know about tucked into the glove compartment, announced her readiness to fly from the proverbial nest.

My stomach flip-flopped as I inspected her tires, looking for the slightest excuse to make her stay another day.

Dana rounded to the driver's side, chuckling. "Mom, please don't dribble your despondency all over my clean car. I. Will. Be. Fine."

Her dad, Liam—aka my beloved—grinned like the besotted fool he was. A perfect portrait of a proud papa. "Rosie, she got the job; now she gets to do what she wants."

Dana folded her arms over her chest. "You taught me to go for the best I could—so my leaving is really all your fault."

The kid got her sarcasm from me; I could hardly

complain. Though I did scrunch my eyes and pantomime a child having a conniption fit.

Dana laughed. A loud bark that set our hounds into howls. She came around the front fender and wrapped me in a big hug. Dana was never small. Even as a baby, she came into the world larger than life, thrashing and screaming, her black hair wild, making her look bigger and badder than she really was.

I hugged her back with every ounce of my fifty-year-old strength.

When her car turned at the end of the lane, I stopped waving and wiped tears from my eyes. Dear Liam held my hand all the way up the front steps.

Once on the porch, I sucked in a breath-taking view of the garden, the green hills, and old-timber woods of the homestead and thanked God, once again, that I had landed in such a lovely spot.

A man wandering down the road caught my eye. *Strange. No one usually strolls these back roads.*

Commotion yanked my attention back to the house.

Juan, my broad-shouldered, eighteen-year-old sunshine child, brought into my life by two miracles—his birthmother's big heart and my husband's absolute trust—bounded out the front door.

I tried to slow his momentum. "Hey, don't go too far. I've got a roast chicken and an apple cobbler planned for dinner tonight."

An apologetic shrug. "I'm heading out—gonna go camping with a few friends."

I flapped my arms helplessly. "In April?"

Logic never stopped Juan. "Hey, Ma, I've worked hard. The guys and I want to get away for a bit, think things over before our next big move."

I scratched my head and glanced at Liam. "By *move*, you mean summer work, right?"

He chuckled.

With a nudge to my husband, I shot one over the bow. “Liam, what do you think?”

Traitorously, Liam grinned. “Have a good time, son.”

Juan squinted in his playful way. “You want to come with us, dad?”

In mock horror, Liam slapped his hand against his chest. “And miss all those long-drawn-out meetings at corporate headquarters?”

Irritated as I was at Liam’s failure to see the point I was trying to make—Juan’s wandering feet and lack of responsibility—suddenly, the idea of camping didn’t seem so silly. “It’d be a lot more fun than the usual L. A. madness, honey. Maybe you could say you’re worn out and need a little R & R. Wouldn’t be a lie exactly.”

Liam chewed his lips as if he was actually considering the idea, but then his gaze strayed to the sky, and I knew that he’d follow the natural course of his destiny. Corporate headquarters called, so he must go. With a hint of despondency, he turned and went inside.

I stayed on the porch, watching Juan gallop to his car and jump in. It was only after Juan’s car had roared down the road that it dawned on me. He took no clothes, no bedding, no tent. *Camping?* My eye.

I sighed as I headed back to the house and faced the roasted chicken that I knew my anxious, hates-to-travel husband wouldn’t eat.

By the time we headed for the airport Friday morning, Liam was in emotional meltdown mode. The man despised corporations and loathed meetings, especially weekend get-better-acquainted gatherings. I slid into the car passenger seat and huffed as he pulled onto the main road, his brow scrunched into tight furrows. How this man managed to rise so high in the tech field was one of the mysteries of life.

I fought my irritation and forced myself to forgive

my husband for missing yet another opportunity to guide our son into responsible manhood, picking my beautiful dinner to pieces, knocking my Easter Lilly off the shelf, and nearly shutting the car door on my hand in his haste to get going so as to get the whole thing over with.

He pretty much strangled the steering wheel in his grip. "If they try to drag me to one of their fancy get-togethers, I'll tell them that I have a fever—"

I watched the countryside fly by and wished I was returning, not leaving. "Say you're sick, and you'll have the entire place hyperventilating. Just tell them you have work to do. They'll respect that."

"They'll laugh and try to set me up with drinks and dates."

I glared out of the corner of my eye.

He kept his eyes on the road.

"You ever consider starting your own multi-million-dollar business and working from home?"

He laughed.

Such a bark, I could almost hear the dogs howl though they were miles away back on the homestead. "I know where Dana gets it."

"What?"

"That laugh. It sounds like a bark."

For the first time since the kids left, Liam smiled. "It's not a bark. It's a hoot."

"You're a hoot." I smiled back; my forgiveness was complete.

By the time I kissed him at the visitor parking lot, he had calmed enough to navigate his way to the departing gate. His long-legged stride maneuvered through the bustling crowd like a heat-seeking missile. His devotion to duty was admirable, even when it annoyed the heck out of me.

The next morning, I rose early, poured myself a cup of hot coffee, and traipsed onto my bedroom porch. I looked around, savoring the glorious view.

No strange man on the road, but odd dreams had interrupted my sleep. Three shadowed figures had loomed before me, gesturing to a dark road ahead.

Shoving the eerie image aside, I breathed deep. I had a whole weekend to myself, and I planned to enjoy every peaceful minute of it.

Home.

There was no place else I'd rather be.

Chapter Two

Even the Birds Stopped Singing

After dressing in jean shorts and a tunic top, I enjoyed a second cup of coffee and a robust breakfast of eggs and toast. Fortified, I ran downstairs and tossed in a load of laundry. Then I scurried back upstairs and wondered why I was in such a hurry. With a reminder to take it easy, I grabbed another cup of coffee and meandered to the roll-top desk in my studio. Like a lady of leisure, I scrolled through my emails and social media.

When the internet flickered off and on around ten o'clock, I didn't think anything of it. We live in farm country, so wild critters sometimes made bad life decisions and interfered with the lines, or storms miles away interrupted service. I glanced outside. No storm. A perfect sunny May first. I shivered for the critter that may have suffered an untimely death.

When my phone chimed from the kitchen counter an hour later, I had just kneaded the last bit of dough for my weekly bread-making and lined up the greased bread pans. My fingers, covered in sticky goo, weren't suited for a technological device at the moment. So, I used my elbow and managed to make the connection.

My sister, Sarah, huffed her words. Must've been jogging, I figured.

"Hey, Kiddo, did your power go off this morning?"

I slapped on the tap water and rinsed my fingers, talking over my shoulder. "Just for a sec." I scowled at the trickle dribbling over my hands. The water pressure was down. Deep inward sigh. Water pressure meant a lot to me. How was I going to take my bedtime shower?

"But it's back on, right?"

The proverbial light bulb clicked on. Power outage

and loss of water pressure. Oh, yeah. Made sense. I peered at the ceiling. The light wasn't on. I glanced to the counter. Nor was the coffee maker. But, silly me, they shouldn't be. It was bright and sunny, and I'd cleaned the coffee maker after my second cup. I glanced at the stove. The clock showed the time but only dimly.

"Hmm…it came back on but—" I ran and flipped the light switch with my wet hand.

My sister broke through. "Hey, I've got another call. It's Bill. Poor guy had to work over the weekend. Better go."

I listened to the click as she hung up, but my eyes stayed fixed to the ceiling. Brown light. Not the bright glare I was used to.

A sound in the distance caught my ear. Horns? Who on earth would be blowing their horn out here? We lived on a dead-end lane, and we never had much traffic, even during planting season.

"Oh, God!" It was an accident. I was sure of it.

But just as suddenly, it stopped. All noise stopped. Even the birds stopped singing. Complete silence.

As if I had been tossed into a pitch-black room, disorientation confused my senses. The whole world appeared to hold its breath, right after a collective gasp.

And then, all hell broke loose.

Chapter Three

Before Things Got Bad

At precisely noon, my brown kitchen light dimmed to black. The clock blinked off. The internet disconnected. The refrigerator stopped humming. The water heater stopped heating. The freezer stopped freezing. And I couldn't get a dial tone on my phone.

Discombobulated, I knew I should be freaking out, but a strange calm flowed over me.

The crunching of a car heading down our gravel lane broke the silence.

I stepped out on the porch and waved.

Our neighbor Josh slowed down. He rolled down the window and came to a stop. A perplexed grin spread over his face. "Something funny's going on, Rosie."

I shrugged his concern away. "Just a power outage. We've had 'em before."

He blinked and shook his head. "I was at the café in town, sitting around with the guys, and Mark said his daughter was having a brownout, just like we were."

Six of my aged hens crossed the driveway, heading for the pine woods behind the woodpile. I watched the collie out of the corner of my eye. She liked to bark at them, thinking she could scare an extra egg loose. "Well, it's no—"

"Mark's daughter lives in Australia."

I snorted in disbelief. "Coincidences do happen."

"So, Ray called his brother in Anchorage, and would you believe it? But they're having power issues too."

Another car came up behind, Josh's wife, Linda. Under normal circumstances, I'd have waved Linda inside for a cup of tea, but the look on her face told me that she knew I wasn't going to be heating a pot of anything soon. Her eyes, wide and scared, sent prickles down my arms. "Hey, Linda. Don't look so worried! You'll scare your husband—"

Linda ran from the car to her husband's cruise and practically tore the driver's side door open. "The power is out in every town and city as far as anyone knows!"

"But you can't know." I shoved fear away as far as I could with every ounce of logic that my brain could muster. "So, there are some power outages across the world. That hardly means that everyone is out. Could be a weird sun thing. A grid failure that knocked out a bunch of places at once. Perhaps there's an internet virus." I shrugged. "Give it a few hours. There's no way we won't get this fixed."

Linda turned on me, and for the first time in our friendship, I realized that I didn't really know her.

"You're being stupid, Rosie. Completely stupid!" She stalked back to her car, yelling over her shoulder, "Get home, honey. We'd better prepare for the worst." She slammed her car door and opened the window as she passed, following Josh. "Just be glad your family is with you, Rosie. My mom is three states away, and Edward is working in Indiana. I just hope to God that they can make their way here before things get bad."

Without the least regard for one of my cats ambling across the road, Linda raced after her husband. I wouldn't be inviting her in for anything any time soon.

But as I made my way toward the house, her words rang in my ears. "Before things get bad..."

Chapter Four

Failed to Send

There was nothing to do but finish making bread. It seemed like the most reasonable course of action. Besides, whole wheat bread straight from the oven soothed even the most troubled soul. I ambled back to the kitchen, put the loaves in the oven, and turned it on low to help them rise.

The oven didn't respond.

I nodded. So okay. Not a brilliant move, but I wasn't about to let my first setback throw me off. I placed the loaves on the counter. They would rise eventually. On impulse, I texted my sister. Sarah always maintained an upbeat disposition under the most trying situations, and besides, I wanted to know what happened to poor Bill. He wasn't really poor. The guy made more money than Liam. I dashed off a quick note.

Failed to send.

Then my heart started to race. I dashed off a text to Liam.

Failed to send.

I tried calling Dana.

Nothing.

I tried Juan.

Nothing again.

I stared at my phone like it had betrayed me...really let me down.

Now I knew what being lost at sea must've felt like. The ground had fallen away, and I had no walls to grab onto. No ceiling. Nothing but a world of non-functioning tools and toys.

I looked at the stovetop to see the time, but, of course, that didn't tell me anything. The house was quiet. Even the road was silent. I walked outside and strolled into the backyard.

The sun perched high, and the birds sang their pretty little heads off. I wanted to talk with someone, but the town was a couple of farm fields away. A long walk.

My stomach clenched into a tight knot.

The big maple outside my bedroom window sported seed pods that helicoptered to the ground. It usually seemed amusing to watch them whirl about and land in masses, covering the ground. But they didn't seem particularly funny now.

I told them the hard truth. "Most of you won't make it to the next season—you realize that, don't you?"

Well, that was morbid.

I shivered in the sun. A big wooden swing set that Liam had arranged under the grape arbor beckoned, so I made my way over and perched on the edge. The garden beds had recently been turned over, and potatoes, onions, even lettuce seeds had been planted. The tomato and pepper plants still sat in flats on the front porch. Liam would get them in next week.

I swallowed.

My fingers inched toward my phone, so I pulled it out, leaned back on the swing, savored the earthy garden scent, and imagined the story I would tell my beloved—once I got ahold of him.

I tapped his number. Nothing. I texted. Failed to send. I squinted in the strong light, trying to make out how much battery power I had left. About half.

I rubbed the back of my neck.

What now?

A couple of vultures circled overhead. *Thanks, guys. Really. Can't you go intimidate someone else?*

I closed my eyes and gave myself a good pep-talk. "I am not going to panic. I refuse to give in to fear. Everything will be fine. They will be home soon, and we'll all laugh about this."

Before I knew it, I had talked myself into a nap.

~~~

An unfamiliar voice calling my name woke me. "Rosie?"

Opening my eyes, my head leaning against the wooden frame, I blinked at the long shadows. I must have fallen into a deep sleep on the large wooden swing of all places. My neck ached. "Uh, yeah?" I craned my head around and saw a figure ambling toward me from the house.

A middle-aged man, probably in his late fifties, headed toward me. Though he could have been Liam's age, fifty-four. Good build but with a tanned, worn face. A neatly clipped beard with streaks of gray matched his short hair. Wearing weathered jeans, a tan shirt, and work shoes, he hefted himself in my direction. *Is he limping? Or does he just have an odd style of walking?*

I stood and brushed imaginary dirt off my slacks.

His eyes lit up. Almost as if he knew me.

"Can I help you?"

He stopped four feet before me, a hint of a smile held in place, though his eyes seemed happy enough. "I was going to ask you that." He jerked his thumb over his shoulder. "In town, a few of us got together and divvied things up so we could check on everyone. See if anyone is alone or needs help."

It all came crashing back to my now, wide-awake mind. The brownout, the power failure, Josh's worried expression, Linda's snooty answer. *Failed to send.* I yanked my phone from my pocket and swiped.

"Won't do you any good." His grey eyes stared at me, concerned. Sad even.
~~~

"It hasn't come back on? That seems strange." Perfectly aware that I was beginning to babble like an incoherent idiot, I swept my gaze around the yard, taking in the elongated shadows. "What time is it?"

He shrugged. "Around six, I suppose."

I nearly fell backward. "That late?" A picture of my dough overflowing the pans crowded out all other thoughts. Ignoring the stranger, I started for the house. "Forgot my bread. Sorry, but I'll have a mess on my hands."

He traipsed after me as if it were the most natural thing in the world.

I hustled up the steps and into the quiet kitchen. Stale air hit me like a sack of dry sand. It felt breathless.

The dough had risen to twice its normal size and oozed over the edges.

I scooped one pan up, dashed the dough back, and thrust it into the oven. Then I shoved in the other three and hit the—

My hand froze in mid-air. *What am I thinking?*

A chuckle turned my attention.

I twirled around, ready to smack the guy. "What's so damn funny?"

He shrugged. Then he grinned and held out his hand. "I'm Ben, by the way. Took me seven attempts before I quit trying to call someone."

I stepped over to the kitchen table and flopped down on the long wooden bench. My hands slapped my thighs, sounding as exasperated as I felt. "So, what did you do then?"

Ben tilted his head and stared right into my soul. "I started praying."

Chapter Five

Light!

My stomach rumbled. So much for the Celestial realm. I considered my guest's quiet form for a moment, then promptly rose to the challenge of finding a quick, nourishing meal that didn't require an engineering degree. I swept past Ben, marched down the porch steps, and crossed the backyard to the woodpile. I grabbed a couple of thick logs, snatched a handful of twigs from the brush pile, and charged into the house.

After assembling a conflagration in the small woodstove that Liam had insisted that we have as a backup, I popped the four limp loaves onto two tiny shelves and closed the door with a sense of accomplishment. Next, I gathered three plastic containers, usually used for juice, and plodded to the prairie grass. I waded through the green tangle and stopped at the well pump. The steel handle glinted in the fading light. I pumped a bit and, sure as shooting, clear water gushed out. Before I could break a sweat, I filled the three containers and then realized that I only had two hands. Plodding back and forth, I managed to get all three containers to the woodstove, where I poured their contents into a large metal pot on the stovetop. I covered it with a lid, checked the fire, added a few more sticks, and nearly pounded my chest with happy satisfaction.

Sitting at the kitchen table, Ben chuckled. To my surprise, he hadn't deemed my marvel of efficiency as a proper excuse to run off and help some helpless neighbor. *Linda perhaps?*

Ben pointed to the chrome refrigerator. "You might want to use what's in there before it goes bad."

I blinked. Images of sour milk, rancid cheese, and

brown lettuce rose in my mind. Before I could stop them, rude words poured forth from my lips. "How long have you been here?"

He glanced at the stopped clock and shrugged. "Don't know, but too long, apparently." He rose to his feet and smiled, tipping his head in a gentleman's goodbye. "Glad to know that you can manage so well. I'll head out now." He paced to the kitchen door and nodded. "If you need me, just call."

I didn't know how to answer. I didn't want to need him. "Thanks. If *you* need *me*, you know where I am." In annoyance at my petulant attitude, I rolled my eyes. *The guy was only trying to help.*

After he'd left, I realized, with a smack to my head, that since the phones didn't work, I couldn't call him. My stomach rumbled—a volcano with dire predictions if I didn't attend to internal matters. I swung open the refrigerator door and decided that warm milk and a peanut butter sandwich would do me a world of good.

Before I finished eating, the sun had set, and darkness settled over the land. No dots of light from the neighbor's house. No haze of color from town. No airplanes blinking like slow-moving stars in the sky.

Where did I leave the lamp oil? I closed my eyes and mentally traveled all over the house. Oh, yes, downstairs in the furnace room on the high shelf. Great. No light to see by. It would be pitch black in there by now. After sweeping the crumbs of my meal into the trash, I laid the dirty plate and glass in the sink. They weren't to run away. Then I squared my shoulders and stumbled down the basement steps.

Oh, God, Liam, where are you? What I wouldn't give to have Juan's eyes twinkling at me, telling me that there's nothing to be afraid of...

I tripped and scared myself silly a half dozen times before I got to the furnace room. Then I felt my way along the wall, bumped into the shelving unit, reached high, tapped around, found the bottle I thought I wanted, clutched it to my chest like a prize, and skittered back up the steps to the nearly dark first floor. The urgency of the situation hit me as I ran for the oil lamp in the living room. Luckily it was perched on the television cabinet, so I didn't have to search around. I unscrewed the top, poured in the oil, adjusted the wick, and nearly had a heart attack. *Do we have any matches?*

"Check the kitchen drawer."

Who said that? Honestly, I wasn't sure if Ben had snuck back into the house or my mind was playing games with me. The strain of the day was beginning to drill fissures into my confidence. Our collie started to howl.

That got me to my feet and into the kitchen. I swiped through the miscellaneous drawer, found the matches, and lit the lamp.

LIGHT!

What a blessed relief. First food and water, now light and warmth.

With a sigh, I carried the lamp upstairs and set it on my end table. Carefully. Too much light and warmth could be a disaster. I didn't want to set the house on fire. No one would come to save me. Except for Ben, theoretically. And what could he do?

I stretched out on the bed, swept my hand where Liam ought to have been, and cried myself to sleep.

Chapter Six

A Day of Impossibilities

Yeah, okay. You got me. I forgot the bread. But since I also forgot the woodstove and let the fire go out, I stood amazed the next day—like a child on Christmas morning—to discover that instead of four burnt-to-a-crisp-loaves, I actually had something eatable waiting for me in the woodstove.

Still dressed in my pajamas—the sudden memory of the bread had shot me out of bed—I gingerly pulled out the pans and placed them on the cool stovetop.

If I hadn't been so bloody miserable missing Liam and the kids, I probably would've done a happy dance. But happy was not to be. Not with my heart constricted and panic ready to seep from the pores of my skin. Liam had an auto-immune disorder, nothing terribly serious, but his body could go into painful flairs without his medication. He'd taken enough for his trip to L. A., but as he had no intention of staying more than the required three days, he probably hadn't packed extra. I tossed a prayer to Heaven. "Please, God, assure me that he took extra. Or that a doctor is near at hand. Or that he meets a pharmacist who happens to carry around extra doses of prednisone."

A gentle breeze wended its way through the open window, fluttering the lacy white curtains. I took that as a sign. Then I snatched up one pan and carried it to the table. I plopped it onto a breadboard, snuck the jam jar from the dark refrigerator, and slathered a slice. "Oh, and"—I prayed between chews—"thanks for this day's bread."

A headache slowed my reaction time, so it took me longer than usual to realize that someone was knocking at my kitchen door. *Ben? Surely not.* I glanced out the window. It couldn't be much after 6:00 AM.

Linda peered, her hands cupped around her eyes, through the storm door. Anxiety lined her face, but then she lifted a thermos like a peace offering. She yelled as if I was on the other side of the Grand Canyon. "I know just what you need!"

Conflicted between the need for my morning coffee and I-haven't-forgotten-yesterday irritation, I opened the screen door and stepped aside.

She pulled a second thermos from behind her back and ambled in. "We'll chat over hot coffee like old times."

My gaze ricocheted around the room.

The morning light streamed through the kitchen windows.

A hen clucked in annoyance at the collie's advances.

Linda sidled over to a chair and plopped down as if the last couple of days had never happened.

My headache sped into overdrive. An image of Ben with his hands folded, concerned, yet strangely peaceful, flittered through my mind. Liam, Juan, and Dana should've been sitting at the table, joking and eating breakfast together. *Oh, God, when will I see them again?*

Linda took a hearty swig from her thermos. "You better drink up. It took Josh an hour to get the fire warm enough to heat up our camp coffee pot. Lucky I still had that old thing. I got the rust out; don't worry."

I unscrewed the top and took a tentative sip. Yowch! It was definitely hot. But the scalding actually felt good going down. Caffeine addict that I was, relief cruised through my body. I sank onto the chair and realized, with only slight discomfort, that Linda was fully dressed while I was still in my morning rumpled condition. My hair undoubtedly looked like I had spent quality time in close proximity to a wind turbine.

Linda didn't seem to mind. Especially not considering the fact that she was drooling, quite literally, at the sight of my home-baked bread.

Being a good Christian woman, I sliced a thick piece, placed it delicately on a napkin, and nudged the jam jar with a strategically placed spoon in her direction. "Eat up. I've got three more."

Linda didn't waste any time.

I shouldn't have been surprised when I heard a tapping on the door, and Josh poked his head into the room. "Hi, uh, is my wife here?"

I glanced over.

A smudge of strawberry jam decorated Linda's cheek. She grinned and waved, frantically chewing the last of her third slice. "Cum-in-hon."

I'll admit right now that Linda wasn't eating alone. I couldn't just slug down the coffee and, besides, it's just plain friendly to eat together.

Once he saw what we were up to, Josh completely agreed. He finished that loaf and part of a second before reality hit. Were the stores still open? Would I be able to get more flour? Or eggs? Or milk? Or anything?

Linda wiped her face and shook her head at my questions. "Nope. Nope and nope. You're out of luck. As are we all. I usually let my winter supplies dwindle down so as to build up fresh stores during the summer. Don't want to end up with thirty jars from an earlier century, like the depression era folks."

I sighed. My headache had abated, but my worries rushed in for the kill. "So, what do we do? Wait it out?"

Josh rubbed his stubbly chin.

Linda stared—finally taking in my rumpled state.

Josh groaned to his feet. "I'm not used to getting up so blasted early, making a fire out back, and heating the coffee camp-style, only to stare at a day of impossibilities." He shuffled to the door. "Thanks for the bread. It'll hold me together to make the tromp to town."

Linda sprang to her feet. "You're going to town, now?"

Josh frowned. "Yeah. I told you. Ben said that we should meet around eight and start making plans. There're old ladies and gents who can't survive by themselves. We'll have to take people in and make everyone comfortable, so no one is left alone." He winked at Rosie. "Despite what the wife says, we got enough coffee to keep us through the hundred year's war." He eyed the last loaves on the woodstove. "And with your baking skills, we'll make do. Just got to figure out what everyone has and what everyone needs."

I glanced at my friend's chagrined expression. Clearly, the coffee supply info was not supposed to be general knowledge. I pressed her hand. "Once Liam and the kids get home, we'll all work together. And everything will be fine."

As if waking from a dream, Linda swiveled around, her eyes growing wide. "Where are they?"

"Liam went to L. A. for a business trip. Juan is off with friends, and Dana is working in St. Louis. Or, at least, she was supposed to be. Right now, she may be sitting in her apartment wondering when the world will get right with itself."

Tears filled Linda's eyes. "Oh, Rosie. I'm so sorry!"

If I had felt worried before, my anxiety level took a turbine lift from her howl.

Josh waved and tried to shush his wife. "Hey, stop! We'll get this sorted out. Juan will make it back soon. Big strong kid that he is. And St. Louis isn't that far. Dana can drive home any time. Walk if she had to. And Liam is..." His words trailed off.

Too far away to walk.

Linda sniffed. "We got troubles, too. Edward is in Indiana, and mom is in a nursing home in Kansas. She's got friends, sure, but she's an old woman with a weak heart. The shock of all this could kill her."

I ran my hand through my rumpled hair, flushed at my bedraggled state, and then went limp with exhaustion. I eyed the last two loaves of bread. Suddenly, I didn't feel neighborly.

Chapter Seven

Gather My Shattered Wits

After finishing the second loaf of bread and pacing around the living room, wringing my hands, I grabbed my banking notebook and took a seriously honest inventory.

The cupboards weren't bare, but they were hardly full either. I realized with chagrin how much food I threw away on a daily basis. In ordinary times, if we didn't feel like leftovers, we gave them to the chickens. Oftentimes bones were given to the dog with plenty of meat still attached. And I had let milk spoil in the refrigerator more times than I could count. Suddenly, waste didn't seem like a minor happenstance. It felt like a crime.

Each day, I took stock and organized whatever supplies I could find. Nothing went to waste. Even old wax was hoarded into jars to be melted down for candles. Torn clothing was sewed up, and broken furniture repaired. I woke with the sun and dragged my weary body to rest soon after dark.

Reading old classics each evening became my newest passion even as my mind wandered across the globe, wondering how people were managing things in different parts of the country and especially in poor countries. *Perhaps the poor finally have the advantage—they know how to make the most with the least. A hard lesson for the rest of us.*

Two weeks later on a rainy Wednesday morning, as I sipped tea at the kitchen counter, I heard footsteps on the kitchen porch and Ben's unique, "Hey-ya!

He tromped through the kitchen door with a satchel slung over his broad shoulders. His face looked older—lined with concern. His eyes a little sadder, as if he had seen troubling things. More troubling than our small-town-techno-disconnect? I wasn't sure.

But he forced a smile as he dug into his bag. "Feel a little like Santa delivering gifts to waiting families." He pulled out a folded envelope. "Hope this helps." Despite the grin, worry lined formed around his eyes.

Gluttonously, I snatched it, tore open the envelope, and unfolded the lined notebook paper.

Hey, Mom,

Hope you're not freaking out. I'm fine. Juan found me, and we're heading home tomorrow bright and early.

Looks like we may be in this primitive state for a while, so Juan came looking for me, and we've decided that we can do more good at home than here. Though we haven't had too much trouble, there are some folks who see this as an opportunity for their own benefit. I got in front of a couple of hoodlums trying to make off with an old man's groceries—the last available in the store. They didn't take too kindly to my interference. Good thing I know how to aim pepper spray. But the old man lost his goods, sad to say. I wasn't a hero. Even Juan sees that simple acts of kindness can get a person killed these days.

We've mapped out a backroad path and hope to make twenty-five miles a day. Should reach home by Saturday. Is dad home yet? Probably not, huh... I shouldn't remind you. Just worried about him.

He'll be fine. He's one of the most resourceful people I know.

Hugs, Mom.

You'll have your kids home in no time.

Love ya,

Dana & Juan

I had no memory of Ben wrapping his arm around my shoulder or how long it took me to cry myself out. I just knew that I hiccupped for hours afterward. Ben didn't say anything. After the gentle hug, a sad-eyed look, and shouldering his mail sack, he was out the door again.

I didn't expect any word from Liam. But I needed to hear from him so badly my body ached with it. Feverous with need, I forced myself to concentrate on making good use of the time before the kids returned.

First off, I knew that I needed sanitized water. Lots of it. That meant heating the woodstove. I needed more wood. So, I spent Wednesday afternoon traipsing through the woods, my few acres of it, and pulling every log and branch I could muster into the backyard. Then I hefted Liam's ax and proceeded to butcher the poor things until they were manageable sizes to stuff into the stove. I stacked the mess as neatly as I could in the metal outbuilding by our old cowshed.

Exhausted, I dropped onto my bed at dusk without so much as changing my filthy clothes. I was too depressed to care. Plus, I had hardly eaten anything. My body and spirit were spent.

Thursday arrived bright and hot. Surprising since it was still only the middle of May. But my growling stomach didn't care about calendars. It cared about food.

Undeterred by my disgusting state of attire, I fumbled to the kitchen and scrounged up a box of oat cereal. I heated water, poured it over the mix, added a tiny dash of cinnamon and a bit of brown sugar, and felt like a queen on holiday. That and a glass of tepid water refreshed me enough to batter down the demon voices in my head.

The idea that Linda might pop by for an unexpected visit hurried my steps as I collected enough water to wash and rinse my body and wash my hair. I still had plenty of shampoo and conditioner, thanks to the fact that Dana loved to try new brands and was always bringing bottles home to experiment with.

I figured that I had two days to gather my shattered wits and get the house into manageable shape before the kids returned and mutiny ensued. Dana always felt that she knew best. Juan, congenially pleasant, went along with whoever was leading. It was Liam who managed to keep all parties on amicable terms.

Without him, how would I'd keep Dana from overruling me in my own house? So, I planned to be sneaky and get everything arranged before she arrived.

I could always use Ben as a character witness. After all, I had survived pretty well on my own. With his support, true. But I didn't need to tell her that.

Chapter Eight

Living in Paradise?

On Thursday afternoon, standing in the middle of a sparkling clean kitchen with bread baking in the oven, I draped a neatly patched kitchen towel over the drying rack and surveyed my domain. I felt so proud of myself. One of the deadly sins, I know, so I should have surmised I was heading for trouble. But the whole house was organized, including the kitchen and the downstairs storage shelves. I had written a complete inventory list and even clipped the hedges, so the house looked neat outside and as well as in.

By five in the afternoon, I was in a pleasant state of exhaustion and treated myself to a tall glass of sun tea. I sat relaxing before the garden under the grape arbor on the rickety old wooden swing, which was still servable if I didn't sway too far.

The sound of a distant siren caught my ear. Was it my imagination, the memory of some cop show where sirens blared across the cityscape? But this was rural countryside. A quiet backwoods world where police hardly bothered to flash their lights, much less sound a siren. If one rolled up close behind, that was signal enough to pull over and find out if you'd surpassed the 30-mph speed limit. A definite no-no that earned a standard ticket and accompanying fine.

The siren continued unabated—no routine practice or alert for a single driver.

My heart began to pound.

I rose and scanned the surrounding farms. No smoke rising. I could safely assume no one's house was on fire. An accident? A call for help?

I squinted at the falling sun. It was still bright, and

I could easily traipse to town and see what was happening. But what good could I do? I'd more likely just get in the way.

Conflict tightening my stomach into knots, I paced back to the house with my empty glass in hand.

With a ball cap on his head, Josh jogged along the road, an ax in one hand.

I blinked and waved. "Hey, you heading to town?"

He nodded, slowing his pace but still moving forward. "Yeah. We arranged the siren as a signal for all able-bodied volunteers to meet up if something important happened."

Not wanting to delay him, I waved him on. "Don't let me slow you down. Just tell me what's going on when you get a chance."

He picked up speed. "Check on Linda if you can. She's not doing great."

"Sure thing!" I called after him, though checking on Linda was last on my list of want-to-dos. I really needed some solid food and a chance to gather my frightened wits. *Oh, heck. Linda is probably chewing her fingers to the bone.*

I ran inside, pulled a bowl of spiced pasta and tuna from the dead refrigerator I used as an airtight storage unit, and speed-walked down the lane. Once at Linda's house, I climbed the porch steps and knocked on the doorframe. "Hey, want to join me for dinner? I brought something tasty."

Linda came to the door, her face red and blotched with the traces of tears still on her cheeks. She wiped her eyes with the back of her hand and forced a determined smile. "I'm not hungry, but I'm glad to see you."

Completely unable to deal with her meltdown, but knowing that my only alternative was to trot home and have my own, I decided to forge ahead with my unwanted charity dinner. "Come on and try a bit. You need to keep your strength up."

After setting two servings of my meager meal, I sat down opposite Linda at her kitchen table and tried to decide if I'd even attempt prayers before eating. What the heck. I made the sign of the cross and then halted when Linda burst into fresh tears.

"She died. Just like I thought she would."

My heart jumped into my throat. "Who?"

"My mom. Got word last night. Some guy at the nursing home wrote—said that the folks are passing at an alarming rate. He can hardly keep up with notifications, much less burials. But, good news, she passed without pain or complaint." Linda peered at me through narrowed eyes. "You don't think someone is helping them to pass along, do you?"

"Oh, God! Why would you think that? It's probably just the shock and the lack of—well, everything. Medicines must be hard to come by and—" I didn't know what else to say. Knowing that the at-risk population was succumbing for a whole range of very good reasons hardly made it more acceptable.

Linda stared at the tabletop, her eyes dry now but her gaze unfocused. "I just don't know what to think. It's like evil has been loosed against everyone. I don't know what terrible thing will happen next." She sniffed and glanced up. "Do we deserve this?"

Dread rose like a monster inside me. I forced it down with the fact that Dana and Juan were due home in the next few days, and they would help us manage through our dark future. Thank Heaven for my kids. "So has Edward started home, yet?"

A shout brought us to our feet. It sounded like Ben's voice.

We ran out to the porch and met Ben at the top of the steps.

Linda reached for my hand and held on tight.

Sucking in air, Ben gripped the railing and caught his breath. "Josh is helping with a water issue in town, but he wanted me to let you know there's been a disturbance."

Linda's hand shot to her chest. "What's that mean?"

Ben shook his head, disbelief in his eyes. "Someone or some crazies decided that this was a good time to blow up the bridges crossing the river. St. Louis is completely cut off."

"What the—?" Fury boiled inside of me. I was already at the end of my tether, and the hope of seeing my kids was the only thing I had to hold onto. Now I didn't know if they had made it into Illinois or not. "When?"

"The news just got to us. It happened a day or so ago. And, yes, some people died. I don't know how many. I don't even know if the people who did it were caught. Not much the police can do at the moment. They were hamstrung before all this started. Now—" He sighed. "God knows."

"They'll call out the army...or the reserves...or whoever," I insisted, as if my certain tone could make it true.

"Hard to call anyone out when phones and gas pumps don't work, and roads are being blocked or blown up. It's mayhem in the cities, from what I've heard."

My knees turned to water, nearly buckling. How could this have happened? Why weren't we ready for something like this? But then, I realized, we couldn't have imagined life without technology. It had come into our lives so completely and taken over. And there had been so much division and hate of late. We could hardly expect people to reasonably band together in bad times when we couldn't get along on an ordinary day.

Linda's voice rose to a squeak. "And the roads to Indiana? Are they still open?"

Ben shrugged. "So far as I know. But it's not safe to travel. Robberies and abductions are out of control." He looked around at the quiet rural scene. "We're living in paradise compared to some."

My heart—clenched in a vice of pain—disagreed. It didn't matter how beautiful the land. If my loved ones were hurting, I was in hell.

Chapter Nine

If I Could Get the Movie Rights

It was nearing the middle of June, and I still didn't know where Liam or the kids were or what was going on in the world, but perhaps I was the lucky one.

After receiving a strange note, Ben had advised Josh and Linda to intercept Edward at Terre Haute, where the boy had been taken for evaluation. Apparently, he was raving about aliens and got violent when people rolled their eyes in skepticism.

The day after they got back with a disheveled, skinny son in tow, they invited me over for a mid-morning snack. I fought down jealousy and cleaned up after a battle in the garden, trying to direct the zucchini vines away from the potato plants. What I said to the tomato plants doesn't bear repeating, though the lettuce was behaving well and offered enough to share when I felt neighborly.

After getting settled on their plush couch in their purple-walled room, I stifled a gag in the rancid air.

The temperatures had rocketed to the low nineties with high humidity. Add the fact that Linda couldn't get used to the idea that with no air conditioning, the inhabitants still had to breathe, so she had to keep windows open, but she often forgot.

I panted like a dog.

Linda perched on the edge of a straight-backed chair in the corner while Josh stood strangely indecisive in the doorway.

Edward paced like a caged animal before the clean fireplace.

Becoming more uncomfortable by the minute, sweat dripped down my back, and prickles spread over my arms at the sight of the twenty-five-year-old man. He had changed so completely; I almost didn't recognize him. I glanced at Linda, then at Josh.

Neither offered a word.

Never one to jump off the deep end, I took tentative steps. "I'm so glad you made it home safe and sound, Edward. I'm rather jealous. My kids were supposed to be back a couple of weeks ago, but...still traveling...I guess." My brave smile died a quick death.

Edward stopped pacing. I've heard of people being frozen in place. An overused literary device that ought to be dropped. But as I stared at Edward, his still form brought the expression to life. He stood with eyes wide and leaning slightly forward, one foot braced for the next step. He halted in place so suddenly, I did the same. Must be some kind of survival thing. One person freezes, and like a scared rabbit, everyone else follows suit. It seemed no one took a breath for a whole minute.

Just as suddenly, Edward knelt before me and grabbed my hands. He stared deep into my eyes. "Oh, God, you could be one of them."

Scared out of my wits, I nearly jumped out of my skin when Josh shouted, "Stop it!"

Linda choked back a sob and rushed over, gripping her son by the shoulders. "Remember what we told you? It's shock, Honey. Just shock. It never really happened. Just a bad dream. But you're home now, and Rosie is our neighbor. Nobody special. Don't worry."

Normally, I would've taken exception to the "nobody special" comment—at least in fun—but at the time, I was too scared to say anything. Edward's glazed expression proclaimed a terrible truth—the boy was surely out of his head.

Edward gripped my hands tighter, clinging like a desperate child. "I'm not worried. But you should be." He glanced back at his mom. "If she's one of them, they'll come looking for her. They'll want her back.

That's probably what happened to Dana." He returned his gaze to my face, earnest and determined. "Though Juan's not yours, is he? Not really. That might be the best thing that ever happened to him–to be free of you."

Feeling like I had been kicked in the gut, I didn't respond. Then Josh pulled Edward to his feet and led him away against stormy protests that he had more to tell me.

Linda scooted over to my side, wringing her hands. "I'm so sorry. He doesn't mean what he's saying. He's just gone so completely out of his head; we can't make sense of him anymore."

Edward's whining voice traveled from the kitchen as he pleaded to be understood. "But she is! I'm sure of it. Her eyes. They see too much. Most people can't see. I bet she can hear too. I bet she knows—"

A door slammed so hard, the house shook.

Linda massaged her fingers as if she needed to get the blood flowing again. I probably looked a little pale. I certainly felt weak as I stared into her face. Worn to the point of exhaustion, there were still traces of recent tears.

Knowing how much I had cried in recent days, I could only imagine her grief now mixed with terror. She had her son back. Or did she? I considered the hardwood floor. "Edward thinks I'm an alien?"

Linda fell back on her heels and then flopped onto the couch, her head resting on the plump edge. "He seems to think that aliens have been around for a while. That somehow, they were planted, or left, or something...and humans and these unknown aliens have been raised together."

"For how long?"

Tears trailed down Linda's face. "Oh, God knows. It's some crazy story that changes every time he tells me about it. If I could get the movie rights, I might be able to sell it, if only humanity wasn't on the verge of extinction."

I would've laughed if I had the strength. But the dam broke, and I joined Linda in tears.

The only good thing about crying together was that after a bit, without any explanation, people often started to laugh together. A sort of involuntary mood shift—a temporary insanity? Don't know.

I only knew that, though I wanted Liam and the kids home more than anything in the world, I suddenly had a whole new concern. *Who will they be when they return?*

Chapter Ten

Winding Road Ahead

I didn't have to wait long.

It may have seemed an eternity, but on Saturday, the nineteenth of June, I heard a familiar tromp of feet climbing up my back porch steps. Two pairs. My beloved kids had returned.

Or so I hoped.

I dashed my hands in the old ice cream bucket of cooled, boiled water that I kept beside the sink, quickly rinsing sticky dough off my fingers. Though I still had a bit of kneading to finish the daily bread, that duty faded to insignificance.

I wiped my eyes, hoping that I'd keep from crying.

First, Dana stepped into the kitchen.

You guessed it; I burst into tears.

Always a little on the plump side with a sweet round face and pink cheeks, long shiny brown hair, and dressed professionally, she now presented a very different image. She'd lost all extra weight, her face lean with high, tight cheekbones. And her hair had been whacked off to ear length. I wondered if she had done it with a machete. Her clothes had certainly seen better days. I pressed my fingers to my lips to suppress an involuntary gasp.

Juan stepped in behind his sister. My overwhelmed gaze immediately recognized his state of malnutrition—bone-thin, ghost-like pallor, sunken cheeks, and dark cavernous circles under his eyes. But when he smiled, my son showed though.

They hesitated only a moment when I held out my arms, aching for a hug.

Sobbing, I gripped each of them, hanging on for dear life, but also, acutely aware that their bones felt sharp against my body.

Dana let go first. As usual, she wanted to get down to business.

"Where's dad?"

I ran my fingers through my short, unruly hair, recognizing the fact that it had come loose from its tie, and I probably looked like a seed pod ready to take flight. What could I say? I shook my head, my gaze dropping to the floor.

Juan plopped down at the table, a burst of a sigh his only reaction.

Dana, on the other hand, took the bossy road. "Have you checked with anyone? Sent letters to L. A. asking about his whereabouts?"

I stared at her. "Letters to L. A.? Who would take them? Who would receive them?"

Dana pounded across the room, stared at the bowl of dough, glanced at me with an unspoken question, and then traipsed to the cabinet. She pulled down two glasses. "You got anything to drink? We've been on the road the last two days straight. It's been madness—fighting for a spot on the ferry, hitchhiking, traipsing down unfamiliar roads, and trying not to get waylaid in the dark."

I glanced at Juan. He looked like he might faint at any moment.

In sudden clarity, I remembered that I was *Mom.* This was my house, and I had managed things quite well despite the devastating circumstances. I wasn't about to waste time jockeying for leadership with my daughter. This was my home, and I was the general in charge.

I swung into action.

"Sit down, and I'll fix lunch." I pulled a pitcher of tepid water from the dark refrigerator and filled the two glasses. I placed them in front of my drooping kids and then pulled toasted homemade bread slices from a tray I kept on a high shelf, slathered them with peanut butter and crushed strawberries, which I had traded for a gallon of cherries, and placed the bounty before their famished eyes.

They ate in relative silence—only their chewing, slurping, and moans signifying the depth of their desperate relief.

Once filled, they looked at me, and exhaustion cried out.

I steered them to their bedrooms, ordered them to take off their clothes, put on something clean, and then lay down and rest for a few hours. We would talk later.

Amazingly, they both obeyed without comment.

After kneading the dough and setting it to rise in the bread pans, I ran upstairs, heard soft snoring, and crept into Juan's room. Comforted by his usual mess, I bundled his strewn rags into my arms. He lay like a child's stick-figure sprawled across his bed, his unkempt hair fanned over his pillow. Despite his emaciation, he was still a handsome young man. Wearing a t-shirt and shorts, his skinny frame sent shudders through my body. I remembered his gaze when our eyes locked in the kitchen. Haunted and grieved, yet still my son. I didn't have to worry about alien abductions with him.

With a grateful sigh, I scurried downstairs and ran outside. I bustled across the knee-length grass and dropped his filthy rags in the burn barrel. *Thank God, we can put this miserable experience behind us.*

Then I marched home and into Dana's room.

Always more composed than Juan, she lay on her back, her eyes closed, and her hands folded on her shrunken stomach. Listening to her steady, even breaths, I stepped across the room and lifted her ragged clothes off the chair. I smiled. She even took care of her rags. *I'm so glad you're home, Sweetheart.*

I had stepped back the way I'd come and clasped the door handle when I heard her say, "We need to talk."

My heart clenched. “Yes, of course. We’ve got a lot of catching up to do.”

“I’ll be leaving again. Soon. We’ve got to find dad.”

I stared at my daughter still prone on her bed. Her eyes remained closed. She hadn’t moved a muscle. Part of me wondered if I had imagined the words.

But her voice rose again, wearily, little more than a sigh. “Later, Mom.”

I shut the door behind me, her clothes clutched to my chest.

Not behind us, just another step on the winding road ahead.

Chapter Eleven

Ponderations

Dana couldn't stand still for a minute. *Perpetual motion machines take notice!*

I sat on the back steps letting a cool front work its magic. For the end of June, the weather was gorgeous. Sunny mornings, warm days with afternoon rainstorms, and blessedly chilly nights. "I wish this would last forever."

Dana stopped pacing under the maple tree and stared at me. Glared really. But who am I to quibble? She had stayed longer than she intended, only because I threatened to get on my knees and beg.

"You're okay *without* Dad?"

I shook my head and tried to wave her comment into oblivion. "That's not what I meant. I was talking about the weather."

Her hands went to her hips. "No arguments; we're going looking for dad. You're not going to give us any trouble, right?"

Juan slipped out my bedroom door and stopped on the top porch step. I didn't see him. But I didn't need to. I knew the sound of my son's footsteps as well as my own heartbeat.

I waited. Juan didn't want to leave home. I knew that, but there was an unspoken understanding that he would go with Dana. He had to. She was going no matter what I said. But she couldn't go alone. And I was hardly fit enough to traipse across an out-of-control country. I'd do better to keep the home fires burning. Literally.

I peered at Dana. She was the same woman who had driven to St. Louis weeks ago, but at the same time, she seemed so altered that I hardly felt comfortable in her presence. There was something she wasn't telling me. And I was weary of not knowing—fighting off the horrors that raged in my mind. So, I countered with a question of my own. "You want to tell me about the aliens?"

She stiffened, her eyes searching in confusion. It was similar to the look that crossed her face when I had detailed Linda's life with Edward—having to keep him away from everyone for fear of what he'd say—was more than just surprise. It was akin to horror. Way too close to home for my comfort.

Not saying anything, Dana backed up closer to the maple tree. Very unusual for her.

Juan tromped down the steps and crouched at my side. He leaned in. "Don't go there, Mom. Really."

I glanced over and met his gaze.

The dead seriousness deep within those brown orbs froze my blood.

Despite his warning, I had to know. "If you can't tell me now, fine. But at some point, I need to know the truth." I stood and sauntered up the back steps, feigning a calm attitude though my insides quaked. *What is that girl hiding?*

"If you guys are leaving in the morning, I'd better make a big supper tonight and get some provisions ready." I glanced over my shoulder. "I may not have cookies and bread enough to last till you get to L. A., but I'll do my best."

Dana called up. "We won't need to go to L. A. Surely, Dad has come some of the way. We'll just ask questions and find out what we can. There's a good chance that we can intercept a letter he sent and get an idea of his location."

"That won't be necessary."

I nearly fell off the back step. Luckily, Juan caught my elbow when I whirled around.

Ben stood between the shed and the porch, staring up at me. His brown eyes holding my own—warm gratitude and a familiar question, “You okay?” in his gaze.

I couldn’t think for the mishmash of emotions that whirled through me.

Ever since the kids had shown up, Ben had stayed out of the way. He knew they were here because Josh had stopped by and given the kids a welcome home present—a bottle of beer he smooched off an old guy who had stocked enough away to last several lifetimes—and was now making quite a profit in the current situation. Josh had mentioned that Ben sent word that as long as the kids were with me, his heart was at ease, and he would take to traveling further afield to “check on things.” Whatever that meant.

My thoughts returned to him frequently. I imagined introducing him to the kids. Wanting to get his reflection on so many things: what he thought about Dana’s personality change, if Juan could assist the men in town, and what about the whole alien thing?

I couldn’t understand why I wasn’t imagining talking to Liam. After all, he was the kids’ father. But as much as I admired my husband, he never was much of a conversationalist. Not about the kids. He could go into astonishing detail about projects, world events, politics even, but when it came to noticing personality changes, internal conflicts, spiritual quagmires, he would usually shrug and do a tilt-head thing. Not his area of expertise, he’d say.

Ben, on the other hand, didn’t say much, but his eyes pondered. His expression would grow thoughtful. Even without words, his simply listening to my ponderations with real interest, comforted me.

So, I stared over the rail, tried not to fall down the steps, and could not think of a blessed thing to say.

Dana rarely had that problem. “Who are you?”

Ben extended his hand and smiled sheepishly. “Sorry. I’m Ben. Just been helping out as I can. I shouldn’t have jumped in like that. Just heard what you said and don't want you heading in the wrong direction." He thrust his hand into the satchel hanging from his shoulder and pulled out three letters.

My heart practically jumped the distance and snatched the letters away.

But Dana was quicker.

She started tearing one envelope open.

Juan shoved past me and pounded down the steps. He ripped the letters from Dana's hands so fast I gasped.

Ben looked equally shocked. At Dana's behavior or Juan's, I wasn't sure.

Juan thrust the letters in my direction. "They have your name on them."

Cautiously, since the world seemed to have shifted under my feet, I climbed down the steps and took the letters. I looked Ben in the eyes. "Thank you. So much." I suddenly understood his need to go "far afield."

I waved them all toward the kitchen side of the house. "Come on in and have some refreshment. The kids can tell you all about their travels—how they managed to catch a ferry across the river, hitched rides, and walked the rest of the way home. Met some interesting people, they say." I blushed. No need to brag. Ben probably knew more wild tales than they could tell.

Dana followed behind while Juan stepped in stride with Ben. Juan asked him something I couldn't hear. Dana's black mood shadowed the whole house.

I was sorry that Juan had been forced to take the letters away. But it was the right thing to do. I was Liam's wife. I needed to read them first, privately. Then I'd share.

Maybe.

Chapter Twelve

Into the Deep End

It was late by the time Ben left, and the kids settled down for a good night's rest before their adventure the next day.

Only then could I sit alone in my room and read Liam's letters. I cried myself to sleep.

The next day, to my everlasting gratitude, Ben offered to go with the kids. He didn't start with that offer, though. Ben was far wilier than I had realized. What came across as boyish innocence masks a deceptively perceptive nature. He outfoxed Dana better than I ever could have.

He had spent the majority of the evening asking her advice, taking her lead. Even glancing her way when I suggested an early bedtime. Almost as if he and she had formed an inside club that knew better than color-in-the-lines-can't-be-too-careful mom.

Juan sat back and luxuriated in someone else taking the burden of conversation off his shoulders, though he did add texture to the stories.

It was Ben who got Dana to share details about their travels.

No one mentioned aliens.

I wished Ben had asked. He might have been able to get away with that line of inquiry when it was clear, I'd have been blown to smithereens for my efforts. Still, it was a great evening. A memory I could snuggle close to, comforting me through the ordeal of reading Liam's letters.

When I heard knocking on the kitchen door at six in the morning, I assumed it was Ben ready to roust the kids out of bed and hit the road for a fresh start before the sun climbed too high. I poured the last of the pancake batter into the frying pan and wiped my hands on a clean towel. “Coming, sir. Right in time for—” I swung open the door.

Josh stared at me through eyes glossy with exhaustion, his body limp and his clothes filthy.

“Josh? What—?”

“Is he here?”

“Who? Ben? He’ll be coming along in a bit.” I glanced out the doorway.

Pushing past me, Josh stumbled into the house and landed on the kitchen bench, his whole body sagging. “No. Edward. Has he come by? Or said anything to you?”

I hadn’t seen hide nor hair of the young man. Didn’t want to either. “No. Everything has been quiet here. Ben and the kids are heading out this morning—”

Josh wavered to his feet. “Don’t!”

I swallowed the fear lodging itself in my throat. “Why?”

This time the knock was followed by the door opening in quick succession. Ben swung into the room, his gaze locking on me. “You okay?”

Footsteps pounded down the stairs, and Dana joined the coffee klatch, though no coffee had been served yet, and I was as confused as hell.

Morphing into the General before her lowly troops, Dana bellowed her first command of the day. “What’s going on here?”

Josh started—his eyes widening.

Ben glanced at me with a look of apology. Perhaps he shouldn’t have encouraged her superiority complex quite so much.

I turned to the wood stove and flipped the last of the pancakes before they burned. “The coffee cups are on the counter, and I made a fresh pot early.” I pointed with my elbow to the tall camping-style coffee pot warming on the shelf above the hot grill.

Like a sleuth who wanted to remain undetected but would dearly enjoy the first brew, Juan slid around me and filled his mug.

I placed the warm platter of pancakes on the kitchen table already set with plates, forks, a small dish of butter, and a jar of homemade jam. "Whatever else is happening, you all need to eat. So, sit down, and we'll catch up after you've got your blood sugar settled."

Dana flapped her hands on her hips. And irate penguin could not have done any better. "For God's sake, Mom. You think we're a bunch of children who can't miss a meal?"

Ben, Juan, and even Josh slid onto the bench and started passing the pancakes along.

Ben chuckled. "Better to eat now than starve later. Especially considering how this day has started."

Growling, Dana plunked down and snatched a pancake in transit to my end of the table.

They all tucked in.

I did the dishes and tried to keep my heart from hammering a hole in my chest.

Finally, Juan wiped his lips and took the leap. "So, what happened to Edward?"

An animal's last gasp could not have sounded more hopeless as what seeped out of Josh. "He's gone with them."

"Who?" Dana and I spoke at the same moment, sounding like an anxious chorus.

"The aliens."

I glanced around to see if anyone else had understood what Josh had just said. Then it dawned on me. As horrified as I had been during the past few weeks, this new plunge into the new normal threw me into the deep end like nothing else had.

It was clear from each of their expressions—they all knew exactly what he meant.

Chapter Thirteen

It's a Deal

Five o'clock on a mid-July evening, and I was ready to spontaneously combust. After rereading them for the fifth time, I left Liam's letters safely tucked away in my bedroom desk drawer and went downstairs. Too many questions and not nearly enough answers.

I invited Linda over for supper, and we slapped flies away as we ate egg salad sandwiches. No chips, of course. Pickles, though. I had finally gotten enough cucumbers to make a decent batch. Vinegar, garlic, a dash of sugar and salt, and lots of dill made us pucker up big time, but they went well with the meal. I even made a blackberry cobbler for dessert. If the flies didn't eat it all first.

I got up and draped a towel over the deep dish. Then I slumped with Monday weariness onto my chair and took another bite of dinner, crunching on the garden lettuce I had added for body since I didn't have many eggs. I glanced at Linda.

She was eating, a good sign. But the dark lines under her eyes, glazed expression, and slow motions bespoke depression's tenacious hold.

"So, have any of your tomatoes ripened yet?" A pertinent question, considering the need for healthy food to be packed away for the long winter. I tried not to think of Laura Ingalls Wilder's version of the Long Winter. Where they nearly starved to death.

Linda dragged her gaze from the flower-rimmed plate and met my gaze. It seemed to take a minute for the question to process. "Oh, no. Not yet. They're getting big, though. All the rain. Just hope they don't rot."

Setting that pleasant image aside, I opened my mouth to try again when she interrupted me—her brows scrunched in concentration.

"What about Liam's letters. You never told me. What did he say?"

I sighed. How much to share? Or how little? A strong desire to make something up—something truly interesting—washed over me like a cool bath. It would be fun to imagine that he had spent the last weeks frantically busy, heroically saving the Pacific coast. But no.

"They weren't terribly fact-filled. The first was ridiculous; he was in complete denial that technology had let him down, let us all down. He insisted that it was some kind of prank. Though by the end of the letter, he seemed to be considering the idea that it might be a nefarious attack by a group of *villainous hackers*. His words, not mine."

"The letters were from early on and just got to you now?"

Mail had been traveling in spurts and drips. All his letters, at least the three that I received, were written in the early days. The second seemed to take the situation more seriously, but he was still convinced that the "snafus" would be cleared up quickly. He made a joke of the fact that everyone in the hotel was swapping medications to manage their various conditions. I cringed at the thought of him trying to substitute something for his daily prednisone. Not the kind of medicine that you want to play merry-go-round with.

I studied Linda, knew she had bared her soul about Edward, and knew I had to tell the truth. "Liam spent the first two letters telling me that the whole thing wasn't really happening. But by the third, he had faced some version of reality. He spent that letter telling me that he loved me and the kids."

Linda clasped my hand and squeezed. We both tried not to cry.

I would have failed miserably had it not been for a

sudden squawking outside the door.

Linda ran into me as we both rushed for the door. Bouncing off each other like school kids racing outside for recess, we managed to make it to the door, disheveled but relatively unharmed.

I shoved a loose swath of stray hair out of my face.

Linda adjusted her shirt.

What we thought we were doing, I hadn't a clue. It just reminded me of how long it had been since anyone came down our dead-end lane.

A buxom woman stood on the front porch with handfuls of birds dangling from her tight grip. I would have burst out laughing if I wasn't so shocked. PETA would not have approved.

Linda didn't care. She giggled.

I could've hugged the strange apparition; such relief and joy ran through me to see even the hint of happiness on my neighbor's face.

I nudged open the screen door, and Linda and I made our appraisal. The good woman before us gave us a once-over as well. Though, she apparently wasn't one to stand on ceremony. Middle-aged, probably siding down the far side of sixty, her gray hair was bundled on top of her head in a way that bespoke long practice and a steady hand. A full-figured gal without the apologetic distracting-dress style, she came across as a woman who didn't care what other people wore or thought she should wear. Loose jeans, a button-down shirt folded back to the elbows, and garden clogs comprised her ensemble.

One of the dangling chickens emitted a decided groan.

Linda whimpered in empathy.

I raised my eyebrows. "Yes?"

"My name is Bolder. Live down a ways from you, but never made an acquaintance. I hear you got some peach trees, and I was wondering if you'd be interested in trading for a few hens?"

To say I was flummoxed would be putting it mildly. "I already have six laying hens, and that's—"

"These here are meat birds, ready for butchering. I hatched out a big brood this year—uncommon lucky how every one of 'em fattened up so well. Never had that happen before." She glanced heavenward.

We followed her gaze and looked up, though no Amen was spoken aloud.

After wringing her hands in helpless bird-empathy, Linda motioned to the henhouse, fenced in near the shed. "You could let them roam with the others, couldn't you? So the blood would stop rushing to their poor little heads."

With a quick nod, the woman assented to this logic and clumped toward the fence, motioning with her chin to my peach arbor made up of four stalwart trees. "My husband and I dearly love peaches, but our best tree blew down last fall, and it'll be sometime before we get another one established. If you could trade us a few bushels for these hens, we'd be indebted to you."

Not being a complete fool, I realized with a cold shudder that I hadn't even considered my meat supply for the winter. I would have enough pickles and salsa to keep the whole county supplied, but without meat, my protein intake would slide off the proverbial cliff. With chagrin, I remembered that my laying hens usually took a vacation during the winter and only laid once in a while—if even that.

"It's a deal!" I may have shouted a tad too eagerly.

Mrs. Bolder didn't seem to mind. After dropping the dazed creatures in the hen yard, she stuck out her hand.

I half expected her to spit on it first to seal our deal. But no, it was a clean exchange. She had a firm grip.

I stared at her steady gaze and realized that I trusted her. Strong and without pretense. I dearly wanted her as a friend.

But she had business to attend to. “Well, I’d best be going then. Delmar is butchering three hogs today, and it’ll be a heck of a job getting everything cut and wrapped up before the ravenous hordes descend.”

Questions flooded my mind: what ravenous hordes? How are you going to store your meat? And could I have some, please?

I glanced at Linda.

With her imploring eyes, she could’ve modeled for a charity flyer.

I sighed. I had every intention of getting answers before the sun went down. But instead, I had even more questions with which to wrangle.

Chapter Fourteen

Humans Among Us

Linda and I returned to our repast and did an amazing job of finishing off the egg salad and an embarrassing amount of the cobbler. Though it was still mid-summer, the days weren't getting longer but slowly shortening, with lingering evenings being the best part of the day.

We decided to sit out on the front porch as the sun set, and the sky turned from pink and yellow into a fiery red. If I had any wine on hand, I would've offered her some. The trees across the road rippled in a gentle breeze, and birds twittered from the electrical lines. I wondered what would happen to those ubiquitous black wires? Would they surge with energy once again someday? Or would they become useless like dead snakes and drop to the ground in imitation of some dystopian novel?

I glanced aside and saw a tear slip down Linda's face. For the first time, really, I cared about her. Not the usual "Hope you're doing well" that we send in quick messages or the "How's everything?" in passing, but the heart-wrenching sensation you get when you feel another's pain. I rubbed her back. "Josh and Edward will be okay." It was an ignorant comment. I knew it, and she knew it.

She swallowed, gulping sobs, and clasped her hands, shaking with pent-up tension. She slid her gaze my way. "You don't know, do you?"

I attempted an easy nonchalance and shrugged. "Tell me."

"Edward wasn't crazy. There are aliens."

That was enough. I didn't want to go any further. Yet, I had to know. Either everyone was going mad or I was way out of the loop. "Aliens? Seriously?"

Her snort should've had a whisky to belt back. "Yeah. They've been here a long time. Since humanity got started, I think."

Whoa! This was a new take on an old theme. "They've been watching us since—when?"

Linda straightened, rubbed her listless arms, and exhaled a long breath. A weary pedagogue having to go round ten with a recalcitrant student. "Not watching. They've been raised with us. Look, I don't know the whole story, but I get the general drift. When life first started on this planet, for a time, everything was just at animal level—you know, fish and birds, creepy crawly things, and then mammals and more adaptable critters. At some point – I have no clue when – there was a divide. Actually, from what I understand, there were several splits. Some of the more intelligent or adaptable animals, pre-human-kind, survived while others fell by the wayside. Was there warfare, a genocide of sorts? Can't say if they were capable of comprehending that sort of thing. But it happened nonetheless."

My gaze strayed to the flowering Rose of Sharon bushes. Their starburst pink flowers with white centers sure looked beautiful. I didn't want an anthropology lesson. I always figured that we could clog the Earth with what we didn't know about our past, and our ever-changing hypothesis about our true origin should be taken with a proverbial grain of salt.

"Anyway..." Linda must've sensed my mood shift. She hurried on. "These alien beings came along and decided—God knows why—to plant their breed among our kind. So, there've been different species of 'humans' growing up on this planet since nearly the beginning."

Was I in a Super-Something movie? "That's ridiculous. We all have the same DNA. Surely we would've noticed if there were different kinds of humans."

Linda shook her head. "You can argue it all you want, but not all humans are the same. Edward said that our DNA has blended, but certain people retain more of the alien species than others. More blue blood, you might say."

My stomach tightened, and my hands twitched. I needed to move. The hoe and a garden shovel lay by the shed. Oh goody, something needed to be organized. The perfect job for right before bed. I jumped to my feet, skittered to the door, and yanked it open. A stray bee, probably thankful for release, buzzed by on its way home.

Not to be outdone in the twitchy department, Linda followed and started pulling the rakes and tools out of the tiny space.

I grabbed the broom. "So, what? The aliens are back and want to take over?" I shoved a bolt of black tarp against the wall and started to sweep dirt out the door.

Linda pressed my shoulder. "The truth? I think that they took over a while ago; they just let us think we were in charge."

I closed my eyes and clenched my jaw against hysteria. Tears or laughter, I could not say.

Linda took the broom from my hand and finished sweeping while I leaned against the wall, praying that I wouldn't get a poison ivy rash or slide to the ground in a faint.

So many images, ideas, and scattered memories flittered through my mind that I could hardly contain my thoughts: Liam's concern over advanced bots that no one understood, algorithms that no longer made sense, massive money in few hands, one-world whispers, sky-rocketing mental illness and dependence on medications, virtual reality replacing family interactions, social media mayhem, and search engine channeling...so many distractions on the edge of my consciousness. I had shoved them aside like batting pesky insects for—how long? Now they rebounded with devastating effect.

I heaved as nausea rose.

Linda pointed to the forsythia bush by the shed. “Go ahead. Throw up. It’s what I did when I finally realized that my son was telling the truth.” She snatched a dust rag hanging from a peg and wiped the shelf.

Forcing my stomach to stay in place, I started returning the tools to their proper places.

Linda’s chuckle wasn’t the least bit humorous. “Funny, you’d think I’d be happy to learn that my boy wasn’t crazy.”

I pressed my hand to my swimming head. “But how can you tell? How can anyone know if we have blended DNA?”

She shook her head and replaced the hoe and rake. “We’re so arrogant. We imagined aliens would be little green men or come with starships blasting with big lasers. We were thinking like children. They aren’t how we imagined them at all. They’re supernatural beings.”

“Oh, God.”

Linda propped the broom in the corner and shut the door. “You got that right.”

Chapter Fifteen

It Was Not to Be

July decided that it wanted to make a name for itself before August elbowed its way to the front of the line, so the temperatures sky-rocketed in the latter half of the month. It was weird to see empty fields where rows of corn and beans used to dominate the summer landscape. *What were the aliens thinking? Humanity needed food to survive. Or was that part of their plan? Kill technology and watch humans die—slowly?*

With a sigh. I surveyed the yard and uncultivated fields. Sure, families had planted gardens, but they were tiny compared to previous years. What the winter would look like, no one could tell. I shuddered to think about the spring. Few people had supplies to last that long.

My zucchini was all but done, and only one giant sunflower lifted its head against the bright blue sky. The lettuce had bolted, though I pulled the last few tough leaves off the thick stems to add garnish to every meal. All the potatoes and onions had been pulled and hauled inside. I was rather proud of the cardboard boxes layered with my homegrown produce. I shifted the boxes onto a dark shelf in the basement, where they were sure to stay dry. I planned to use lots of white onions when I made salsa. I was just waiting for the tomatoes to do their thing and ripen in a big bunch to make a canning day worth the effort.

Feeling a tad lonesome, I turned back to the house and let the oldest cat, Earl, inside where he slept on the chair in the living room most days. His rickety old body could hardly jump the distance, and I knew there'd be a day when he'd fall back to the floor in cat disbelief. But for now, he was someone to talk to. Even if I knew full well that he was dreaming his last days away.

With the high humidity and heat, I didn't feel terribly hungry mid-week. I had spent most of the day clearing out the back shed in the expectation that when Liam and the kids did make it home, we'd have to think seriously about getting a couple of cows and expanding our chicken run. We'd have to store hay for the winter and figure out how to grow our own feed grain. Other people were making adaptions—necessitating the use of every old barn and shed in the county. Wood and metal for roofing were going for a premium price. I had to make the most of what I had. And that meant clearing out the dusty space and shoring up the frame so it wouldn't collapse over the winter.

Hot, sticky, and fearing the revenge the spiders would perpetrate on me for wiping out their webs, I trudged into the kitchen, planning on nothing more than tomato slices and a glass of water for dinner.

I nearly had a heart attack when I saw a man sitting at my kitchen table. My first thought was that Liam had finally made it home, but then I realized that this guy was much too young.

"Edward?"

He stood up and faced me, not a hint of a smile on his face. "I've got bad news, Mrs. Oxley."

I swallowed and gripped the kitchen counter. I didn't want him to tell me *anything*. I couldn't believe a word he said. The man wasn't trustworthy, no matter what his mom said. "Does Linda know that you're here?"

He shook his head, his gaze steady, unflinching. "I came to see you first. I'll check in on them next."

Them? How detached had this guy become?

"You should see your mom and dad now. Linda's been so worried. And Josh—"

"Your husband died last night."

Volcanic fury filled me, lava rocks roaring to the surface. I was so ready to hit this bratty, know-it-all kid who thought he could prance into my kitchen unannounced and bald-faced lie to me. I stomped my foot and shouted, meaning every word, though I hardly realized that I had it in me to spew such hate-filled wrath. "Get out of here, you punk! Go play alien games with your friends and stay the hell away from my house. If you really want to help—leave your parents alone too. They don't need your asinine insanity!"

He stepped forward, his arms hanging limp at his side. "I found Dana and Ben—they buried him in a field in Missouri. He almost made it home. But he wasn't made for this world, not like it is now. He got an infection. Never told his traveling companions how bad it was, not till it was too late."

I might as well have been taking psychedelics, the way the room started spinning. I nearly fell to the floor. Coming out of nowhere, Josh grabbed me by the elbow and half-carried me to the kitchen table. Stunned, I couldn't even process the fact that Josh was in my kitchen.

I just stared ahead, my brain shutting out every logical thought.

Voices murmured and, at some point, I was directed to the living room where I stretched out on the couch.

Steps echoed across the room. A door slammed shut. A hand held a wet rag to my forehead. I closed my eyes and prayed for death to take me.

It was not to be.

Sometime in the night, I awoke to the sound of the rocker creaking across the room. Groggy and sick to my stomach, I struggled to rise onto my elbow.

"Don't get up, Rosie. It's still early, and there's nothing to be done for a few hours yet."

Linda? "What are you doing here?"

"Josh heard that Edward was back and followed him across town. He listened in the doorway and ran inside when he heard the news. Got me so I could keep an eye on you through the night."

My mouth felt as parched as an old paintbrush. "Is he crazy? Edward, I mean."

A soft sigh and a murmur. "No, I'm afraid not. It's the world that's gone crazy. Or it has been for a while, but we refused to see it."

I let that sink in. The memory of the boy's words hit me again. But this time, I could hear them. And I could believe them. "It's true—about Liam?"

"Yes, honey. I'm so sorry. He got sick while walking along the highway—don't know why exactly. No doctors around to diagnose him. Or he never asked. But the trek across the country without proper food, the strain of worry, the heat, it was all too much. Edward said he was out of his head, couldn't talk straight. It was a mercy, really, that you didn't see him like that."

A mercy? Had everyone gone insane? "I would've liked to have been with him in his last moments. Held his hand. Told him that I loved him."

Another sigh. "He knew. Dana was there. She told him, and he died with a smile on his lips, she said."

Bull shit! I wanted to scream. That happy scenario was a story Dana made up to make everything seem better. To write the narrative she wanted. A man who loves his wife and kids doesn't die on the highway far from home with a smile on his lips!

I clenched my jaw and bit back scathing fury.

The rocking resumed. "Dana is meeting up with Juan this side of St. Louis, and they should be home the day after tomorrow. Thank God, Josh got home in time to help with Edward. The boy isn't feeling well at all—and no wonder.

Questions ricocheted around my brain, but

exhaustion finally took the field, and I dropped off to sleep. I honestly didn't care if I ever woke up.

Chapter Sixteen

I Had a Spirit

I sweat buckets in the kitchen as the temperatures continued to zigzag right into August, but a storm front promised cooler temperatures. At least, that's what Ben said when he lugged in garden bounty with Dana and Juan following at his heels like lost puppies.

I was too depressed to care even if an arctic winter was in the forecast. I couldn't wrap my mind around the fact that I'd never see Liam again. That I had missed his last days, his last moments. His burial.

Swiping away the threat of tears, I forced myself back to the task at hand.

The tomatoes and peppers had ripened nicely, and with the pile of onions I had stored away, I had enough fresh ingredients—with bartered cilantro from a family in town—to make a decent batch of salsa. Luckily, I had stocked up on vinegar last year. The extra gallon came in handy with all the pickling and canning I was doing.

After washing the five-gallons' worth of tomatoes, I sat on the hardwood bench at the kitchen table, cut off the bad parts, and sliced the juicy red goodness into tiny pieces. Next, I worked on the pile of bright red and green peppers, and finally, I faced the dreaded onions. I didn't need a reason to cry. I had plenty.

Flies swarmed the pots and dove into my face, adding to my frustrations. Hot and sticky with a storm front pushing the humidity into the unbearable zone, I worked mechanically. Focusing on one step at a time.

Grab an onion by the tail.

Slice one side.

Peel.

Chop into rings.

Turn and chop into cubes.

Drop the pile into the pot.

Wipe my stinging eyes.

Repeat.

"You want some help?"

I looked up. There was Dana reaching for a knife and settling across from me at the table. Guess I didn't need to answer. She could read my mind. Or so she thought.

I sniffed back stinging tears and lost my rhythm. I was supposed to be cubing, but I went to the sink and splashed water on my face instead.

After patting my eyes dry with a towel, I looked at my daughter. Why was I so angry at her? She hadn't done anything wrong. In fact, she had done everything right. Found her brother. Made her way home. Gone off to search for her dad and found him. And buried him.

"Mom? You okay?"

I stared at the onions. I wanted to hate them. But I couldn't. "No. Not okay."

Dana stopped chopping. "Me neither." She had dropped her head onto her chest, and I could tell by the heaving action that she was either sobbing silently or about to throw up. Or both.

Maternal instinct to the rescue, I ran over and hugged her, my arms wrapping her hunched shoulders as best I could from the awkward angle. I let myself free from my tightly wound emotional straitjacket. We both did.

The onions saw it all.

Two grown women sobbing in front of a table full of vegetables.

A throat being cleared brought me to my senses.

Dana nearly bolted from the table.

Juan's eyes were tearful, and I wondered if he

wanted to join us in our crying-jag, but he just shook his head wordlessly.

Dana stood up and maneuvered around the table. She marched up to her brother and in some sort of big-sister silent command, she stared him into an explanation.

"Edward died a few minutes ago."

"What!" I couldn't believe my ears. The kids had just gotten home a week ago, and Edward, despite his previous ravings, seemed to be doing better. He was calmer and didn't mention aliens anymore. Linda had asked me to bring over some salsa the first chance I got, to help Edward rebuild his strength.

It was on my to-do list. "Make salsa and bring a jar to Linda." She'd have to give it to her son herself. I was still annoyed that he had told me about Liam the way he did. Stupid kid should've waited for—what? I wasn't sure. Till it wouldn't hurt so much to hear?

"What happened?" Dana stroked Juan's back.

Irritated again, I stepped over and closed in. Juan was my son. She didn't have to mother him. "I'm so sorry, Juan. Another shock after so many."

Juan kept shaking his head. "It's not me. I didn't know Edward that well. I mean, we never hung out together or anything. It's Josh and Linda. This has hit them hard."

Dana sighed. "Of course, it has. Must be hell to lose a child."

I peered at my daughter. What did she know of it?

"At least they got to be together before he passed." Small comfort, but it was more than I got with Liam.

A knock on the door pulled Dana away. I took over the mothering role and rubbed Juan's back.

He edged away. "It's okay, Mom. Really. I'm not upset. Just, you'll have to do something about Linda. This might be more than she can take."

Ben stepped into the room. His gaze appraised the scene, taking in every detail at once. I probably could've asked him what spice jars were empty, and he would've given me an accurate answer.

He nodded. "Sorry I didn't come by earlier. It's been a rough time for a lot of people, and I knew you had your kids."

Confusion swirled my brain. I grabbed onto recent events and thrust it to the surface. "What happened to Edward?"

"He mixed some homemade brew with sleeping medicine someone had given him. Not a good combination."

I should've staggered, but I had been hit so hard of late that this didn't knock me off my feet as it would have a couple of months ago. I looked into his eyes. "Linda?"

"Josh is with her, and they've got word that Linda's aunt Sophia is on her way. She's one amazing lady—she'll do Linda the world of good."

I let that information go into the later box. "What about Edward being an alien? I thought he was protected or something."

"He wasn't an alien. Or not much of one. Like the seed that sprang up in rocky soil...he just couldn't grow true."

Dana nodded as if she understood.

Juan peered at the floor, listening but not commenting with words or body language.

I looked over my shoulder.

Vegetables waited for no one. Especially not in this heat.

I turned back to Ben, ready to focus on something I could manage. "If you help with the onions, I'll give you a free jar of homemade salsa."

Juan snorted. "You'd give him five jars anyway, Mom."

I made a snarly face at Juan.

Ben laughed and lifted his hands in surrender. "I happen to be the world's best onion slicer. Won awards for my chopping skills too."

Dana nudged him toward the table. "Go on then, big talker. Show us your stuff."

Ben rubbed his strong, compact hands together, his grin weary but alive. "Give me a mission—and I'll get it done."

Relief flooded me at the idea of Ben at the table with the kids. It wasn't the same as having the family intact, but it was close. Remarkably close.

As I watched Ben and the kids jostle and tease, my spirits lifted just a tiny bit. For the first time since I heard about Liam's death, I remembered that I had a spirit.

Chapter Seventeen

Aunt Sophia

If there are five stages of grief: denial, anger, bargaining, depression, and acceptance, I did most of them twice and out of order. First, I couldn't believe that Liam was dead. Then I got mad at Edward for telling me. I was annoyed with Dana for her part to play, and by the end of the week, I figured I'd just go ahead and accept reality.

Next, depression set in. My answer to that was to forget the whole thing—just refuse to think about it. I tore every wedding photo off the wall, packed most of Liam's clothes and personal items off to the charity center in town, tucked my wedding ring into a jewelry box, and stuffed it at the back of a high shelf. From then on, I'd focused on what needed to be done. I completely forgot bargaining. Liam was undoubtedly in a better place, and I had no wish to join him yet. So, no bargains.

At that point, after anger had stomped my heart into submission, depression and the broiling August sun turned me into a wobbly noodle.

If it hadn't been for the arrival of Linda's aunt Sophia, I don't know what I would've done.

Sophia arrived on a hot August morning traipsing down our lane dressed in jeans, a flannel shirt with the sleeves rolled up, sandals, and a weathered farm cap on her head. She used a walking stick. Not just any walking stick. It looked very much like a shepherd's staff.

I happened to be in the backyard picking ripe tomatoes and peppers, arranging the day's plan in my mind. Another batch of salsa was on the horizon, as was fresh bread and a blackberry pie. The meat birds were fattening out quite nicely, and I worried about butchering day. Without an ounce of hatchet skills, I couldn't imagine how I was going to transform the ugly creatures into dinnertime specials.

When I heard a whistling tune, I glanced up in time to see this strange apparition pass by. I followed her with my gaze, saw her turn in at Linda's house, and knew that this must be the amazing Aunt Sophia. I'd never seen such a perfectly packed human being before. About four foot ten, with short grey hair, a stocky build, thick fingers, and a broad face, she wasn't exactly inspiring. Which is probably why I underestimated her.

I shouldn't have.

Doesn't look too amazing to me. I thought of poor Linda lying unresponsive on her bed. *You have no idea what you're in for, woman.*

I gathered the green and red bounty into my apron and toddled off to the kitchen. I dearly felt for Linda, but I didn't have an ounce of emotional energy to spare.

By noon, a small batch of fresh salsa sat on the table next to freshly baked bread, while the last blackberry pie of the season rested on the stovetop, covered by a dishtowel to keep the offending flies away.

Feeling rather smug, I shouldn't have been so surprised when Ben and the kids crashed into the house like a football team intent on scoring a touchdown. They happened to be filthy.

I arranged my face into my most intimidating glare. "What on earth have you been doing?"

A shared gaze between them, and then to my uncomprehending mind, the three burst into laughter.

I hated being left on the outside—as if the joke was somehow on me. "What?" I wasn't laughing. Not even smiling.

Juan plopped down on a kitchen stool with a groan. “We met Aunt Sophia!”

Ben traipsed to the sink and poured dribbles of water over his hands, rubbed them with a sliver of homemade soap, and then rinsed, ever careful of the water supply.

Dana leaned on the sink next to him, undoubtedly waiting her turn.

Curiosity got the better of me. “What’s she like? I saw her pass this morning. Tiny thing, she’ll have her hands full getting Linda out of bed, much less getting her to eat anything; I’ve tried.”

Ben shot Edward a look. Dana snorted.

Now, I was seriously ticked-off.

As Ben dried his hands on a towel, he faced me. He wasn’t smiling anymore. “Linda’s up and doing better. In fact, she’s invited us over for dinner.”

Good Lord, it wasn’t possible! The woman had been knocked off her feet with grief to the point where I feared for her life. “How can that be?”

Juan lifted a limp hand. “She had us working all morning. Got plans for the whole town. You aren’t the only one invited.”

I turned to Dana, hoping that she could translate this nonsense I was hearing into something comprehensible.

Dana waved a hand over her hot face. “I need something to drink first.”

Ben sat at the table, pulled the bread plate over, sliced a piece, and dipped the crust into the dish of salsa. He hummed in satisfaction.

Juan eyed the pie but followed Ben’s example and cut the next slice.

After swallowing a full glass of water, Dana wiped glistening sweat from her forehead and smiled broadly. “Aunt Sophia is just what this town needs, Mom. An organizer with lots of good sense. She’s been to three towns already and got them up and running so that they're prepared for winter. Word is—it's going to be a doozy this year. We're lucky she came."

Juan talked around a chew. "She gave Linda what she needed—a reason to live."

Exhaling a long-suffering sigh, I peered at Ben.

He nodded. "Yep. She's a full-blooded alien. And Dana's right. We're lucky she came."

I don't think I'd ever felt more terrified in my life.

Chapter Eighteen

Not Strong Enough, Yet

Full-blooded alien, what the hell did that mean? Was Aunt Sophia wearing a human costume? Was she a little green creature under a humble womanly visage? And even more importantly, what on earth was I going to bring for dinner?

As the shadows got to the middle of the big maple tree out front, Ben stepped in through the kitchen door and offered a mock salute. “Ready for new worlds, Captain?”

Grimacing, I folded the dishrag on the edge of the sink. “Go ahead and laugh now. Get it out of your system before we leave.”

Earlier, I had hauled bucketfuls of water from the well, soaped and rinsed my whole body, dressed in my only clean slacks and button-up blouse (I had reserved them for a formal event: a funeral, wedding, or baptism), and in my clean attire faced the man I hardly recognized. “Gosh, you look nice.”

After a courtly bow, he smiled. “You too.”

Dressed in a pair of fresh jeans and sporting a pressed sky-blue shirt, Ben wasn’t laughing. Though the crinkles around his eyes suggested that he hadn’t lost his sense of humor, apparently, he took this dinner invitation as seriously as I did.

“I know it’s just dinner with the neighbors, but you said she was a full-blooded-something, and heck, that could mean royalty. I figure it’s best to err on the side of caution. She could have troops waiting in the wings to squash the unwashed.”

Ben laughed.

I shook my head at my blushing face as I fiddled with the kitchen towel, wrapping it around my sumptuous—I hoped—apple pie. “You know more about the whole alien situation; I'm stumbling in the dark."

"You're doing fine."

I stopped at the doorway. "How do you know?"

For the first time since I had known him, Ben got physical with me. He took the pie dish from my hands, set it on the counter, and pulled me after him out the door and across the yard to the refurbished shed. He pushed the door open and nudged me inside.

Curious as a cat with six more lives, I allowed myself to be directed. Perhaps I should have been afraid of a man I had only known for a few months, but Ben never alarmed me. Rather I always felt comforted or amused in his presence.

Suddenly, I was feeling something quite different. Not fear but excitement, as if I was on the edge of an amazing discovery, something that would change my life forever.

The dim interior didn't allow much light, but it was cooler than I had imagined. Being under the canopy of a mid-sized elm and an ancient maple set in a hillside, the resulting shady spot with earthen background, created a natural cooling chamber. A fact I would appreciate in the coming years.

Ben placed one hand on the wall by my head and leaned in, his face only inches from my own.

As I was wedged between his arm and the door, I couldn't shift away. I pretended a calm I didn't feel and raised an eyebrow.

Ben's voice dropped lower than his usual custom. "Because I'm one too."

As my heart dropped to my knees, I closed my eyes. I dearly wanted to close my ears as well. "Oh, no, Ben. Don't say what can't be unsaid."

A strangled laugh caught my attention, and I opened my eyes.

"I've wanted to tell you a hundred times, but you

were never ready. But now, I think you have to grow up and come to understand our true identity."

Beyond feeling as if I had just been tossed into an icy ocean amid twenty-foot waves, I was fine. I lurched forward, trying to bust my way loose. "Our? As in me too?" I brushed past his arm and made for the door. "Don't try this alien-identity thing on me! I'm perfectly happy as a simple Earthling. No need to build myself up with false grandeur."

Ben grabbed my arm and held on. "You've always known you were different. Admit it. You called it being sensitive. An overachiever. A good listener. That's how you knew things that others never picked up on. That's why everyone trusts you. How you manage to get so much done. Your dreams that are more real than reality. You go places and meet others that few people ever can—"

Horrified by his words, I shook my arm free. "Let go, Ben. I mean it. I want nothing to do with Edward's delusions or our current culture's obsession. I'm just me. Not smart. Not exceptional. Just a quiet stay-at-home mom who does her part. And makes lots of mistakes." I squinted in the dim light and looked him square in the eye. I nearly stumbled over the sincerity I saw there.

Grief crushed my heart into a quivering mess. Ben was such a wonderful guy. He could be eighty percent star-dust, and I'd value him for the sweet, hard-working, determined gentleman he was. But getting me to join the alien club wasn't going to fly. "Look, Ben, let's forget this. Words can't be unsaid, but they can be ignored. I'm going to ignore this and go to dinner at my neighbor's house."

"But Aunt Sophia is—"

"Aunt Sophia can be an elf from old Ireland for all I care. I don't need her. I'm just going to make Linda and Josh happy and satisfy my stupid curiosity." Tears formed in my eyes, and I resented them. I didn't want to show up on their doorstep looking like a love-struck teen who had been on a bad date. "But I need you. My friend. Please, don't go alien on me. I don't know if I could stand that."

With a sigh, Ben took my hand and clasped it tightly. "Okay. You're right. Timing is everything. Right now, we need to think about Linda and Josh and the rest of this town."

Though that wasn't exactly the response I had hoped for, his strong fingers around mine enveloped my whole body in indescribable comfort. *I'm not strong enough yet* flashed through my mind. And deep down, I knew I was right.

And so was Ben.

"Let's go meet Aunt Sophia."

Chapter Nineteen

The Devil's Minion

Linda answered the door and accepted my pie with a quiet smile. She wasn't acting like the half-crazed cult worshiper I feared. She waved Ben and me inside with a soft chuckle. "The kids got here before you. Something about orders from on high." She stopped at the kitchen counter and laid the pie next to an assortment of dishes. "Go on into the living room. There's not much left to do, and nearly everyone is here."

Feeling oddly out of sorts, I was grateful that Ben strode at my side into the living room, which had been arranged into a presentation room with the large French doors opening into the backyard. A table with a glass of water, some loose papers, pens, some colored markers, and a bowl of unshelled peanuts stood to the right. A large crowd mingled in the yard and flowed through the house, stopping and chatting in casual interaction.

Before I had time to puzzle out the peanuts, I saw the little woman working her way through the yard and into the room, one hand tapping her forehead as if trying to jog loose a thought. She called out, "Juan, can you—?"

Juan hurried over.

She leaned in with whispered instructions.

Juan nodded, then ran off.

Marveling at her authoritative yet gentle manner, I simply observed, fascinated.

She looked up and met my gaze.

If I expected something electric, I was disappointed. She strode over, a busy woman anxious to make my acquaintance.

Without the usual formalities, she didn't offer a

handshake. She just stopped before me and offered a smile. "You must be Rosie. I've heard a lot about you."

I tripped over the words, "Nothing bad, I hope," and gurgled incoherently.

Ben snorted with a comfortable laugh. "Thanks for inviting us, Sophia."

Sophia nodded. "Glad you could come. Linda has been through a lot—the world turned upside down, losing her mom, then her son." She shook her head in grief-stricken contemplation for a moment but brightened almost instantly as she stared me right in the eye. "Oh, before I forget, I met your sister, Sarah, and her husband, Bill. Despite everything, they're doing well. Funny that we crossed paths so early on, and then I should meet up with you here."

Shock thrilled through my body. I had thought of Sarah and Bill often, but after Liam died, I couldn't bear to imagine what might have happened to them. They lived in Wyoming. Hardly expecting to hear from them, I nearly choked in surprise.

Ben took a step closer—to do the Heimlich maneuver or restrain me—I wasn't sure.

I stared at Sophia. "You met Sarah? How is she? And Bill—they're together?"

"Doing well, both of them." A twinkle entered Sarah's eye. "I suspect she's pregnant but doesn't want to say anything yet. But healthy and thriving. Their whole community came together as soon as the lights went out and, naturally, being farmers and ranchers, they have a lot of know-how to help them through. I didn't stay long."

My head spinning, I tried to imagine this tiny personage traipsing across the country. "Where're you from—originally?"

Sophia shrugged. "It's a long story. Not a very happy one, so I'll leave it alone." She glanced aside as Linda entered the room. "We're not actually related, you know. Her dad was from a first marriage. I'm adopted, sort of, from a second. We were brother and sister in the eyes of the law, not DNA. But we always treated each other as family. There are things that go dccper than blood."

Linda glanced around, a lost puppy looking for a warm lap.

Sophia jogged over and ushered Linda to the table with quick instructions.

With a hesitant smile, Linda started sorting through the peanuts.

More befuddled than ever, I let Ben usher me toward the backyard, where people were beginning to assemble in some sort of order. Juan and Dana were helping to get everyone organized.

Conversations buzzed all around me with disturbing signs of condolences to family members for those who had passed on recently. How many people had died? I tried to gauge the number, but these were painful, private matters and could hardly force my way in and ask detailed questions.

In a short time, we were arranged in a half-circle facing Sophia, who stood on the threshold, her hands clasped and her eyeglasses sparkling in the afternoon light.

"Hello, everyone. Glad so many of you could make it out here. We thought of doing this in town, but as things are now, smaller is better."

Alarm bells rang in my mind.

Ben's hand rested on my back, and I was glad for his solid strength.

"As you all know, we have got a lot of work to prepare for winter. So, the community leaders decided to break our town into groups of a hundred, more or less, depending on family sizes. As this group settled out, there are eighteen family groups with a scattering of singles. You all live within walking or biking distance of each other. Our plan for today is to get a list of our greatest needs and figure out who can assist whom to make final preparations for winter. It's going to be a hard one, by all accounts. We don't have the usual luxuries, and with a shortage of medical supplies, it's very important that everyone stay as healthy as possible. I ask in all earnestness that no one take any unnecessary risks." She pointed to the bowl of peanuts. "I brought fresh peanuts for anyone interested in growing them next year. They're a hearty and nutritious food source, so feel free to get your share. Linda is passing them out according to family size."

Appreciative murmuring rose through the group.

Sophia looked around. "Juan, are you ready?"

Juan lifted his arm. "Yep, I'll take my group—the Allmans, the Colter family, Peter James, Quinn-Sui family, and Mr. and Mrs. Jacob."

People began to shuffle about, attempting to get to Juan, who soon led the straggling group beyond the line of apple trees.

Dana then lifted her arm and called for another group.

Josh started his list.

Then another man called out names, and more shuffling carried people to far corners of the property.

I turned and faced Ben. "What about us?"

Sophia tapped me on the shoulder.

I looked at her, confusion warring with dread.

"You and Ben are with me. We've got more serious matters to attend to."

A laugh bubbled in tune with circus music playing in my mind. "What's more serious than surviving winter?"

Sophia met Ben's intense gaze. "Dakuri is coming."

For the first time, I saw shock in Ben's eyes, followed by horror.

I swallowed, afraid to ask what I knew I must. "Who?"

Ben lifted his gaze to the fading sky. "The devil's minion."

I wanted to joke. "Well, if he's only a minion, he can't be too terrible." But the look on both their faces told me that I wouldn't be laughing for long.

Chapter Twenty

Who You Want to Become?

Two weeks later, I once again stood in Linda's living room. This time, I pouted. I had been looking forward to a mild end of the summer and an early autumn, so the blazing heat at the last of August, leading into September, took me by surprise. Especially since this was the first year that I ever had to go without air conditioning.

My worst fears realized, people were dropping like flies, and that was not a pretty image. During all the sorting and planning that folks did over the weekend, Sophia let me know that I had a very special job. She called it the Tobia Service.

Basically, I was supposed to figure out where to bury all the bodies.

I faced Sophia's congenial face with my hands on my hips, frustration filling every crevice of my being. "Why me? And can we get back to the Dakuri fellow you mentioned?"

The whole day there had been a million interruptions with questions about everything from how to contact the fire department and get medical attention to how to stop mildew from turning onions into bags of soggy mush.

Everyone was busy as bees at harvest time. Too busy to deal with my moody attitude, Sophia left me with my new assignment title and headed off to settle a squabble between the Allmans and the Colters concerning a shared well. The kids were mentoring groups, ticking off lists, and getting volunteers, while Ben worked with Josh on a half-completed building project.

Linda sat at the table and handed out her precious

sacks of peanuts.

With nothing better to do, I smoothed my ruffled feathers strolled over.

She handed me a bag with a shy smile.

Didn't she know me anymore? Or did I not know her?

I pulled a kitchen chair close and sat at her side, clutching my sack. "You doing okay?"

Linda shrugged. "I'll never be the same. Some wounds go too deep to truly heal." She peered at me. "But you know that already, don't you?"

Taken aback, I frowned. A throb started at the back of my head. "What's that mean?"

"You're one of their kind." She shrugged again. "Course, you still have free will. You can reject it."

"God Almighty, what are you talking about?"

"It's what Edward told us. Long ago, aliens came and seeded this planet with their kind. Everyone grew up together, but the special ones were gifted with abilities. A higher nature—or something. Edward wasn't one. But he wanted to be. It nearly drove him mad." Her eyes, dry but unfocused, stared at the throng on her doorstep. "I don't know why it should've bothered him so much. I'm not one—nor is Josh. But that doesn't make us any less valuable. We have free will too. And we can grow, if given the chance."

I rubbed the back of my neck. Part of me wanted to throw the bag of peanuts across the room. The whole notion was insane. "There aren't two different kinds of humans, Linda! It's a crazy story people are making up to deal with the stress of being without technology."

Linda turned and stared into my eyes. "There are many kinds of people, Rosie. Always have been."

"I mean human and alien."

"We're all human. Just some come from a higher place. More developed."

"Get off it. No one here can fly at the speed of light, blast buildings with their bare hands, or leap tall buildings. It's all comic book stuff."

Linda stood and huffed. "Golly, Rosie, are you stuck back there?" She gathered the last of the peanut bags and started for the door. "I'm going to pass these out, so they don't go to waste." She shook her head. "When Jesus said that people could move mountains, he wasn't talking about shifting Mount Kilimanjaro. Some people improve the world with their creative ideas or kill it with their selfish desires. Miracles happen all the time. Healings or holocausts. Most of us just live ordinary lives. But some people have no idea how extraordinary they really are. They change the whole world." She peered over her shoulder as she stood on the threshold. "You might want to figure out who you are—who you want to become."

The last rays of the day swallowed her in an evening glow.

Ben flashed into my mind. Who was he?

Dana bounced over and tapped my shoulder, nearly making me shriek.

"Sheesh, Mom. Calm down. We aren't at war—yet." She jerked her thumb backward. "Ben wants to know if he can stay the night. Sophia has Edward's bedroom, and it looks like they're going to be taking in two elderly couples who won't make it through the winter on their own."

The temperatures had dropped considerably since the sun hit the horizon, and a refreshing breeze blew through the house. My shoulders relaxed. "Yes, of course." I peered at her through the rising darkness. "Are we *taking in* anyone?"

Dana laughed. "Just Ben so far. But he'll be plenty!" She pointed to Juan and a clutch of stoop-shouldered people gathered in the distance. "We're going to stop by their houses and see what needs to be organized for the move. But don't worry, Juan bartered for a really huge candle—think it came from a church—so we'll see our way home in the dark."

I meant to ask what she bartered with, but Ben sidled up as I searched for any sign of Sophia. I took his offered arm. "I want to ask what she meant about my Tobia service-thing. What the heck am I supposed to do? I don't know anything about funerals, burials, or cemeteries." Pressure had built behind my eyes like a volcano ready to explode.

Apparently sensing my discomfort, or perhaps it was the fact that I kept rubbing my neck, Ben patted my hand as he tucked my arm closer and started home. "You need a wee sip of my homemade spiced wine and a good night's sleep."

Rattling between irritation and supplication, I whined, "I don't drink. Never wanted to. But I do need answers."

Sophia stood on the roadside, chatting with Linda. They both smiled in the twilight.

I barged up. "Sorry, but I'll never get to sleep wondering what I'm supposed to be doing—especially since I don't think I can do it."

Linda chuckled and pressed Sophia's arm. "See you in the morning. I'm heading off to dreamland." She ambled across the yard, met Josh halfway, and they strolled into the house together.

The crowd had disbursed, and night had fallen in all its star-strewn glory.

Sophia faced me though I couldn't see her face clearly, just a glinting outline of her body. Like a glow.

"The man who took care of the cemetery records put everything online five years ago. That's not available to us now, of course, but there were also paper records. So, we just need you to check every time someone dies and make sure that we have an open gravesite—no cremations these days—to bury the person."

"Why can't the last guy do it? He knows better than I do, right?"

With a soft touch, Ben rubbed my slumped shoulders. "He died two weeks ago."

I sighed. "Well, it's just record keeping, right? It shouldn't be too hard." My whole body relaxed at Ben's touch. "Tobia didn't keep all that busy, surely."

Sophia held Ben's gaze a little too long for my comfort.

Suddenly, I didn't have to ask. I knew.

Tobia had been kept very busy, indeed.

Chapter Twenty-One

On Top of Mount Stupidity

Cemeteries scared me for a very good reason. I only knew where about half of the bodies were buried. The rest was pure guesswork. I trembled at the idea of discovering at a graveside service with a grieving family standing around that the burial site I thought was free and clear was actually occupied.

I stood under the great oak trees at Calvary Cemetery, clutching an old map and tried my darndest to find the burial sites for three people I knew had been buried there. How did I know? Because their relatives sent obituaries published in the early part of the century, acclaiming the names and death dates of three individuals buried at our Cemetery.

But I couldn't find them. No paper trail and no tombstones. I walked the blessed yard, covering about five thousand grave sites twice. And I wasn't doing it again.

So, when a gentleman dressed in clean slacks, a brilliant white shirt, and a fancy leather jacket ambled up and offered to assist, I didn't tell him to get lost. I nearly fell at his feet in adoration.

For some reason, he seemed to find my state of near despair amusing. "I'm Jake Uri. My family has lived here for generations, so I know where the clans liked to cluster." He wiggled his eyebrows for emphasis.

Relieved from my state of hysteria, I laughed and waved my arms toward the vast tombstone cluttered expanse. "Thomas Reynolds, Faith Cuthbert-Reynolds, and daughter Lura Jones. If you can find them, you get a gold star."

He shrugged. "Neither gold nor stars have ever been my thing. But I'm happy to assist." He strolled to the rock driveway, paced to the cornerstone, and then counted his steps along the edge. Once he reached the Lovelace tombstone, he turned right, counted his steps again and then stopped three feet away from the Harrison's tombstone. A grassy space about five sites wide lay before his feet. He pointed to the front end. "The three bodies are right there. Sites four and five are open." He glanced at me. "How many sites does the family need?"

"Two."

"Works out well then. Where did you get the obituaries?"

His narrowed gaze seemed to search my integrity while I really should have been questioning his accuracy.

"Grace, the granddaughter of Lura, sent them along with instructions that her aunt and uncle could have the last two sites on this plot. Josie and Greg died within three days of each other, and the family wants the burials done and over with ASAP."

Jake savored this information like a judge considering pie slices at the state fair. "Yes. A remarkable family. They were very close as children then had a falling out over an inheritance. Ironic that they'll be stuck with each other through eternity."

Discomfort wormed its way through my mind. "Perhaps they made up—that's why they're sharing the family plot."

"They hated each other to the bitter end. Well-deserved too. Bratty women married to overbearing men who couldn't handle a nightcap with dignity."

Oh boy.

With the information in hand, I could direct James, our gravedigger, and get on to other matters. Like figuring out where Ben came from. That had become my secret obsession.

I thanked Jake with all the sincerity of a woman who had been spared pain and humiliation and returned home to the savory scent of roast beef with garlic, onions, and potatoes stewing in a pot. The additional aroma of bread baking sent my salivary glands into overdrive.

Ben stood at the counter, chopping tomatoes into a bowl filled with mixed greens. He had planted a second crop of lettuce, spinach, and kale in the backyard, giving us two more months of fresh greens. I was ever so grateful.

I dropped my cemetery notebook on the shelf by the door and plodded to the sink for a glass of water. Traipsing across a cemetery, even on a beautiful September afternoon, was thirsty work.

Ben continued chopping but gestured to the defunct refrigerator with his elbow. “Made a gallon of lemonade. Though it’s not sweet. Sugar is just too dear these days, and I figure the lemon flavors the water just as well.”

Bouncing between rapture and curiosity, I sallied forth, retrieved a glass, pulled the container from the dark interior, and poured myself a healthy serving. I had to hold myself back from slurping it down in a few gulps. I wiped my dripping mouth and peered at this miraculous man. “Where did you learn to cook? And do the hundred and one things you know how to do?” Greedily, I poured myself another glass. “Seriously, what amazing stalk did you sprout from? You’ve mentioned plenty of places you’ve traveled through and cities you’ve lived in, but where are your people from—exactly?”

Ben parried his cooking spoon through the air in mock battle. “By people, you inquire about my clan, my tribe, perhaps?”

“Your DNA of origin, if you want to get technical.”

All amusement fled from Ben’s eyes. “Sure you want to know?”

Doubt shadowed my happiness, but curiosity kept nudging me toward the light. “I can’t find anyone with your family name in the records. You're—"

A loud knock on the door drowned out my words.

I swung open the kitchen door and found Mrs. Bolder standing on my back porch with her hands on her hips, a storm about to blow.

"You kill them yet?"

I honestly didn't know what to say. On the one hand, I hadn't killed anyone that I could recall, but on the other hand, I wasn't sure that was the answer she wanted to hear. I merely shook my head in innocent denial, relieved to feel Ben come up behind me.

Mrs. Bolder was not pleased. Her entire countenance darkened, and it was already pretty threatening. "You'd better. They'll be tough as all get out soon, if they're not already. Muscle is no good, you see. You want 'em fat and tender."

I wasn't sure what horror flick I had stepped into, but I sure as shoot'en wasn't going to keep pretending that I knew where our conversation was going. "Who am I supposed to kill?"

Ben laughed and stepped around me. "The hens she gave you." He nodded a welcome and ushered the good woman into the kitchen.

Of course, I felt like an idiot. I had completely forgotten the hens. I fed them in the morning, and Juan closed them in the enlarged henhouse each evening. The collie kept only half an eye on them, as she followed the layers like a devoted admirer, hoping for a protein snack undoubtedly.

Perhaps I'd simply wanted to ignore the fact that having meat birds meant that there must be a butchering day. Not a pleasant prospect.

Dana stumped into the house, offered a wave to Mrs. Bolder, and took over the conversation. "Hey, glad you're here. We've got to do something about those fat birds. There're more than we need, so I think we could do some trading with folks. I was thinking—"

Panic took over my mouth. "I can't chop heads off, pluck feathers, or gut anything. I don't know the first thing about it. And I have not the slightest desire to learn!" So there. I took my stand. Alone. On top of mount stupidity.

Dana stared at me a brief moment and then returned to Mrs. Bolder. "Monday is going to be cool and dry, so we could gather a group and get the job done in no time. Might even have a picnic out back for fun."

The black mood dissipated, and Mrs. Bolder smiled, showing a gap where an eye tooth should have been. "My idea exactly. My husband will help. Josh and Ben are old hands, and I can get a couple others. You and your brother can help out and learn how it's done." She glanced at me and sniffed. "She can make a pie or something."

Once the deal was made and everyone was feeling chummy, I invited Mrs. Bolder to stay for dinner.

"Can't. Got supper for my old man on the grill. He caught some lake fish, and we're going to bring some to Ma, who lives in town now."

Honestly, I thought the woman in front of me was older than the hills, so the idea that her mom was still alive knocked my timeline out of whack. "How old is your ma, if I might ask."

"Hundred two. Though she don't look a day over eighty. Got good genes in the family. I'm aiming for a hundred three."

With that gauntlet toss, our visitor whirled away.

I turned around and caught Juan going right for the hot loaf of bread Ben had just set out. Dana nearly beat him to it, and they enjoyed a sibling squabble.

I sidled up to Ben and nudged him in the ribs. "Don't think I forgot my question. I still want to know where you came from."

Ben sighed as he set the pot roast on the table. "I was born aboard ship."

Juan and Dana sat down and prepared to dive into the feast.

Lifting my hands, I insisted on grace before meals. We all bowed our heads and prayed.

As everyone got their suppers assembled, I sucked in a satisfied breath. "On board ship, eh? That must've been hard on your mom. I hope there was a doctor available. Were you docked or out at sea?"

Ben held his spoonful with a steady hand and looked me right in the eye. "We were galaxies away, sailing through the distant universe." Then he took a bit and chewed meditatively, remembering his shipmates undoubtedly.

I glanced from Juan to Dana, who ate with calm relish, unconcerned that we had just entered the *Twilight Zone.*

I shoved my bowl away and decided I'd never ask another question so long as I lived.

Chapter Twenty-Two

If You'd Be Wise

Autumn hardly got started before the temperatures dropped, and cold winds swirled their way across the land. The garden had died back to the point where we were only getting a few measly tomatoes and a handful of scrawny kale a day. Still, I coveted fresh food wherever I could get it.

In a fit of inspiration, Juan had sprouted herb plants in his back bedroom, and they were thriving, so we still had some dill, thyme, oregano, sage, mint, basil, and tarragon. He couldn't get the rosemary to stay alive, which I never could either, so I duly sympathized, while I rejoiced at his ingenuity.

The mint was a godsend as coffee, and black tea were harder to come by. Mint tea offered a soothing alternative and, without the sugar, I added to my usual drinks, presented a healthy lifestyle choice I probably never would have accepted otherwise.

Added to this, we had a new arrival show up at our backdoor. A black and white kitten with a funny face that Dana promptly named Luna, which—because of the kitten's antics—I frequently embellished with the more robust name of Lunatic.

Dana and Juan turned out to be surprisingly copacetic with the whole butchering scene. Considering the fact that Dana had always wrinkled her nose when I cut up meat for dinner, and Juan never seemed to notice if he was eating a spare rib or a veggie burger, so long as he could swallow it down and run off with his friends, they both got into the Chicken Day event as if it were a fall festival.

Only later did I put the whole Thanksgiving feast and fun theme together. It wasn't a national holiday, but it sure felt like one when seventeen people showed up at the back door with sharpened knives, scrubbed buckets, gallons of boiled water, and sealed containers ready to tote their precious cargo home. Several families planned on canning the chicken meat, while others had improvised a dried-meat-jerky type thing to preserve their protein harvests.

As predicted, I served pie.

After the rush of preparation and then the day itself, I was exhausted. I was also harboring deep-seated discontent. What did Ben mean when he said he'd been born on a spaceship? Not a funny joke. But he hadn't laughed about it either. He just refused to discuss the matter further while we ricocheted between preparing for our Chicken Day Extravaganza and panic that we'd mess up and the birds would go to waste.

I need not have worried. Ms. Bolder and her crew knew exactly what to do. I just had to stay out of the way and direct them to mint tea and deep-dish apple pies when it was all over.

That Monday night after the final cleanup, I collapsed on the couch and closed my eyes, hoping to cleanse the sight and the smell of chicken guts from my senses.

"Lazing about, I see."

I peeked out of one eye. The other was too tired to respond.

Ben stood before me, a self-satisfied twinkle in his eyes. Nudging me over, he plunked down on the sagging couch.

I mumbled, "How's a woman supposed to collapse in peace around here?"

He sat there, one hand gently caressing my weary arm.

Enough was soon too much, and I dragged my body to a partially upright position. I stared at him through my bleary vision. "I haven't forgotten, you know."

He dropped his hand on his lap and held my gaze. “I know.”

“It wasn’t funny.”

“Wasn’t meant to be.”

Though I had been up before the sun and my body ached with weariness from deep cleaning the house from top to bottom, preparing for the unexpected community event, and making six pies, suddenly, I felt wide awake. I straightened and brushed my disheveled hair from my eyes. “You’re sticking to your story?”

“I am.”

“I’d like to beat you up, you know.”

A grimace turned grin told me how much he feared my punch. “Are you ready to listen and hear what I have to say?”

Okay, I deserved that. I had to steady myself. The couch wasn’t moving, but my heart was flip-flopping all over the place. “Yes.”

Ben lifted my feet and scooted back on the couch, repositioning my legs onto his lap. It was a rather odd position, strangely intimate, yet not intrusive.

He leaned back and stretched, readying himself for a good storytelling.

I snuggled into the couch pillows and forced myself to relax. I made up my mind, without knowing how, to really hear him this time and not hold back.

Apparently sensing the opportune moment, Ben launched into his epic tale. “My parents were from another solar system, a place not so different from this one. I don’t know the whole story, but a series of clans, family groups—what have you—left my home world over a period of many generations. I am not certain why they left other than some terrible threat forced them to leave. The images I carry in my mind, like a kind of symbolic art, reference an explosion. Solar destruction, a catastrophic war, diminished resources, an epidemic outbreak—one event or a succession of events—I don't know. All I am certain of is that my parents died after coming here."

"But we've no record of a ship landing and dropping off emigrants from outer space. I'm pretty sure that would've made the news."

"Not if it happened 500 years ago. In the 1500s, many strange things happened, and if someone reported a ship appearing in the sky and landing on Earth, he'd have been laughed at or sent to an asylum.

I swallowed hard, trying to absorb the implications of what he had just said. "You're 500 years old?"

"There about, give or take a few years. I stayed young for a very long time—handed about like an idiot child who'd never grow up. No one kept track. Not even me."

Nausea rose inside of me like boiling lava. How could this man—a man I had come to admire and trust—be so completely different from who I had imagined? "*What* are you?"

He exhaled a long, weary breath. "I'm not an Earth human or completely alien. I'm something of a mix. I have a much longer life span than you, but we share a great deal of DNA. I come from a distant world, but I belong here. This is my home, as far as I am concerned. Humanity, varied as it might be, is my family. Some of us have advanced characteristics, while others are far less developed. Even among my own people, there was a spectrum. Some noble souls. Some nearly demonic or certainly influenced by the demonic."

A shudder worked through my tense body. "You believe in demons. Seriously?"

Sadness filled his eyes. "I do. And if you'd be wise, so would you."

A new wave of exhaustion enveloped me. This was too much to take in at once. I needed to sleep, to escape this fresh shock to my already strained system. I closed my eyes. But then, beyond my comprehension, I reached for Ben's hand, held it close to my weary heart, and responded with more honesty than I normally dared, "I'm so glad you're here."

Chapter Twenty-Three

Can't Live a Lie

I hardly expected September to heat up as it did, but I was often surprised by the obvious. Every year, when the leaves started to turn yellow and fall from the trees, I would think that autumn had come early. I would get excited just dreaming of cooler days and brisk nights.

Then a stretch of hot days with bright blue skies contrasting against the dying fields would send me into a fit of melancholy. It was like when it poured rain from black thunderclouds, and then the sun came out at the end of the day. The ground was slippery with wet leaves, and the humidity climbed, but the sun beckoned as if it were strolling weather. Such strange contrasts and contradictions.

Finally, in the latter half of September, the weather broke, and mild rain fell from a grey sky—sending a cool breeze, whispering true autumn melodies.

I had shored up all the outbuildings, though I wanted to drag out a few of our precious haybales to make a sturdy shelter for the collie and our kitty companions. My shoulder was aching from energetic floor scrubbing, but I needed to keep working—keep my mind from wandering, thinking about the world, life, and what it all meant. The box I had kept my universe in was far too small these days.

Despite my curiosity, I didn't delve any deeper into Ben's foreign family roots. I almost brought it up a couple of times, but he seemed to make himself scarce as soon as I paused with a question forming on my lips.

Dana, on the other hand, was going out of her way to hang around. I wasn't sure if she was worried about me or if she had a bomb to drop and wasn't sure when to let it loose. She had that nervous quality about her, like when a person was trying to ingratiate themselves into patriarchal favor in order to inherit the family jewels.

Except I had no treasure other than her and Juan, and she knew that perfectly well.

Being a quiet guy, Juan seemed to prefer the company of other men. He worked on projects with Ben and joined the volunteer rescue group in town. It was another of Sophia's brilliant ideas—to expand and train more people from the original firefighter-paramedics department. It seemed to be working out well, and Juan developed a passion for it. Really brought him alive. I could hardly believe that this was the same kid who wanted nothing more than to hang out with friends in order to decide his "next big move" for summer fun. Now, he bustled about learning life-saving skills and organized our small town into survival mode under the leadership of Ben and Sophia, of course.

I was still just Mom.

"Mom?"

Monday morning and Dana already had me jumping out of my skin.

Rain drizzled from clouds the night before and at the break of day, but now blue sky broke through, and the sun felt warm on the skin.

I peered out the kitchen window. Our tomato and pepper plants had outdone themselves and were producing to beat the band. Which meant that I had some valuable trade goods. Which also meant that I was making hamburgers with lots of eggs and breadcrumbs added to stretch the meat for dinner. I planned a salad using the last scraps of lettuce. *I really should get out there and pick again.*

Dana flopped her arm around my shoulder. "There are still some cherry tomatoes to pick. You want to help me?"

Holding back a perplexed head-shake, I refused to admit that in times past, I was the one suggesting a joint garden venture. What kind of role reversal was going on here? Why were my kids suddenly turning from children to my caretakers? Had I gone senile and not noticed?

I shoved aside the unpleasant realization that if I was senile, I'd be the last to know and gathered up two beat-up ice-cream buckets.

We sallied forth.

In a completely unexpected move, Dana nudged my arm and grinned with a mischievous twinkle in her eyes. "Wanna race?"

I almost said, "Do I look like an idiot?" But instead, I took off at full gallop. Pretty good for an old gal, I must say.

I won.

Only because Dana slipped in the grass and did an awkward belly flop.

The good sport that she was, she just laughed, and we picked cherry tomatoes with joyful abandon. The first carefree moments I'd had in ages.

Once back in the kitchen, we started to sort and clean the pile of luscious, red goodness.

Dana and I sat at the kitchen table and created piles. One for home canning. One for trade. One for this week's meals. I was puckering for a happy hum when Dana cleared her throat.

"Dad didn't suffer too much. Just so you know."

My mood plunged into the abyss. So much guilt had hounded my steps, that I'd refused to even think about Liam's last moments. I hadn't asked for details. I decided to be satisfied with the bald facts. He tried to get home but died on the way. *How* wasn't all that important?

Or was it?

I shoved the bucket aside and propped my head on my hand. Part of me realized that Dana had as much need to tell me what happened as I needed to know the truth. We had both kept busy staying alive and holding that terrible day at bay.

She kept sorting tomatoes, turning each fruit with an examining eye before committing it to the right pile. "You know how dad needed his medication to keep the flare-ups under control, especially when he was under stress?"

I nodded. I knew well indeed. At times Liam had hardly been able to walk for the pain in his joints. But with a good diet, proper rest, and regular doses of his meds, he did wonderfully well. Medication was always a weak spot—left him so vulnerable without it.

"Well, you know Dad. When someone else needed the same meds, he shared his. And he didn't ask for help. But as his condition deteriorated, someone gave him something to help with the pain. Lots of stuff was going around. Juan and I saw it all over the city, even in the early days. It was like a joke. Get high long enough to skip the bad parts, and everyone would get sober when the nightmare was over."

Tears welled in my eyes at the thought of Liam in pain—desperate enough to take whatever was offered.

"Some of the stuff going around wasn't pure—not medication at all, really."

I closed my eyes, and tears overflowed.

"By the time we got there, no one could've saved him. It was a miracle that Juan and I found him at all and were able to see him even for a few minutes before he died." Dana reached over and took my hand. "I'm so sorry, Mom, but I made up the part about dad dying with a smile on his lips. I thought that would make you feel better. But weird as it is, I haven't been able to live the lie. Even such a well-intended lie."

I forced out my words. "How did he die?"

“In pain. With a grimace.” Dana broke down sobbing, unlike anything I’d ever heard from her before. She howled like a mortally wounded animal.

When I tried to wrap my arm around her, she thrashed and knocked a bucket of tomatoes to the floor.

But suddenly, I wasn’t a feeble, senile old mom. I was Rosie—the daughter who had taken care of her parents till their natural deaths years before, the wife who managed Liam’s sickness even when he tried to ignore it, the mom who had raised her kids with love and devotion, the woman who had held things together long before the world fell apart. I collected Dana’s broken spirit in a fierce hug, and after a moment, she grabbed me back like a drowning woman hanging onto a lifeline.

Then Ben walked in.

Chapter Twenty-Four

He's Trouble

Ben understood the dynamics of my family well enough, by this time, to let us wipe our eyes and gather our wits before attempting any conversation. In fact, he was sensitive enough to allow us the whole evening to recover from our resurrected grief. By morning, we were able to joke at the breakfast table with Juan, who seemed bent out of shape by a minuscule incident at the cemetery.

Dana guzzled her coffee and plowed through her eggs and wheat toast as if she planned to spend the day wrestling a grizzly bear.

Ben sat back and sipped his coffee, listening to Juan as he whined like a child.

I pared apples, hoping to dry slices in the autumn sunshine—preparing them to be packed away for a winter delight. I only listened with half an ear. Keeping my fingers whole was my current objective.

Juan shoved his cup and plate aside. "He's freaky—got an evil eye or something. So blasted sure of himself, even when he's tromping right over the security regs we set up. Yet he pretends to be on our side. Such a hypocrite!"

Dana swallowed a large bite and nodded in vigorous agreement. "He's strange, all right. Got ulterior motives for everything. I heard he's got his own trading system, which involves a big profit—for himself."

I glanced up. Dana and Juan had been so agreeable of late that this angry tone caught my attention.

Ben and I locked gazes before he swiveled his attention back to Juan.

"I'd just like to know why he was digging around in the cemetery last night. Ghoulish, if you ask me."

Juan jerked away from the table and stood up.

Disturbed by the image, I nicked my finger and swore under my breath.

Ever composed, Ben nudged a dishcloth in my direction.

Swinging my attention full on Juan, I ignored the frown, undoubtedly making me look angrier than I felt. "Who was digging around the cemetery?"

Juan placed his dishes in the sink and poured a cupful of clean water over them, leaving them to soak. "That stupid Mr. Uri. A class act with no substance. He's a faker and a liar."

I glanced at Dana.

She copied her brother and added her dishes to the growing pile. "I don't know if he's a total idiot or a malevolent charlatan. But Mr. Jake Uri is definitely not a team player."

I dumped my apple slices into the bucket, placed the paring knife aside, and tried to understand what my kids were talking about. "You mean to tell me that Jake Uri was digging in the cemetery without telling me? I'm the one who keeps the records. No one is supposed to dig up or bury anyone or anything without letting me know."

Ben stood and stacked the dirty dishes to one side, while he filled the sink with water. "Sophia has been keeping her eyes on him. She already knows that he's trouble. Just not sure what to do about it. Yet."

Suddenly outraged at the thought that anyone had been messing about in my cemetery, I propped my hands on my hips. "Well, I think I need to have a little chat with Jake. He was as friendly as pie to me when we met some weeks back. And I really need a direct answer. He can't dig out there. It might set others to thinking that they can bury—well, gosh knows!"

Ben added a tiny bit of soft soap to the water and swished it about. He leveled his gaze at me. "Don't go confronting that guy by yourself. He's not what he seems." He nodded at Juan and Dana. "They've got his number, alright."

Squirming with indignation at the idea that I couldn't manage one middle-aged gent by myself, I snorted my disgust, fully aware of the fact that I had a hard time confronting the cat that insisted on sleeping in my flower pot.

Dana slapped Juan on the shoulder. "We'd better hurry. Sophia has a drill planned for this morning, and then we're supposed to help the Hendersons pump their septic system." She offered an encouraging grin to Juan.

Juan grimaced in return. "Oh, boy, so much fun in one day. I don't know how I'll stand it."

Ben chuckled as he soaped and rinsed each dish in turn.

I grabbed a kitchen towel and started to unload the drying rack. I nudged Ben. "So cute how they support each other, isn't it?"

Ben rolled his eyes. "They're adorable."

We worked in silence, though the laying hens suddenly ruffled and cackled as if a wolf were at the door.

I peered out the window but saw nothing unusual.

After the last dish was put neatly into the cabinet, I pointed to my bucket and raised my eyebrows. "Want to help me set these to dry in a safe place so we can have apple pie this winter?"

As affable as ever, Ben's blue eyes twinkled as he grabbed the bucket by the handle. "You sure know how to sweet-talk a guy."

I wrinkled my nose at the recent exchange as we started for the door. "At least I have some faith in your abilities. Better than you all have in mine. I'm not an idiot. I think I could handle the likes of—"

The chickens squawked prodigiously.

My heart racing, I ran ahead and scrambled out the door and right into Jake Uri.

Funny, thing, when I glanced over my shoulder, Ben didn't seem the least surprised.

Chapter Twenty-Five

A New World Order

Now that I stood face to face with Mr. Uri, my confidence sagged.

Jake smiled as if he didn't have a care in the world.

Ben sidled around us and toted my apple bucket to the picnic bench, where he started laying out the slices in neat rows.

I dragged my gaze off my friend and focused on the unaccountable person in front of me. He wore an impeccably clean white t-shirt, neatly pressed tan shorts, and gleaming leather sandals. Perfectly dressed for a summer day. And though the temps were unseasonably warm, it still seemed a bit off. But his ingratiating tip of the head and half-bow offered old-school manners that I'd always admired.

"Well, hello, Mr. Uri. Speak of the Devil!" I laughed to take the sting off the unfortunate phrase. "We were just talking about you."

I had a mental image of me trying to pull my foot out of my mouth. But to my relief, Jake only laughed.

"Have you, now?" His gaze swiveled to Ben and stayed there for an uncomfortably long moment. Then he turned back and gleamed at me. "I wanted to stop by and discuss some important opportunities that you may not be aware of during these trying days."

"Opportunities?" Good golly, I couldn't imagine anything close to an opportunity in our depressed times, but I was certainly willing to become better informed. I gestured to the house. "Please, come in and have a cup of tea. I've even managed to hold back a few slices of banana bread for a snack if you'd care for some."

"Sounds delightful."

Wow, this guy was a charmer. My heart flip-flopped. To my shame, I didn't even give Ben a second thought as I led Jake inside.

The man had a discerning eye, and he quickly appraised pretty much all my furniture, knickknacks, and even the pictures on the wall with an expert's sharp opinion. He dismissed my grandmother's woven fruit basket and the St. Michael the Archangel painting with a flick of the hand, but he gushed over my dad's first-edition history books. "I'd give you a fair price for these, Rosie. They really should go where they can be properly admired, not stuck on a dusty shelf where no one realizes their true worth."

My initial temptation was quickly dismissed when I realized that money couldn't buy a family heirloom. I simply shrugged. Though the thought that I was doing something vaguely selfish heckled my reserve. I returned to the kitchen and placed the kettle on to boil.

"Oh, please, don't bother with that. I can't stay, really. I just wanted to share some news with you, since I think you're one of the few people in this town who can honestly appreciate the value of true preservation."

Contrary thoughts ricocheted through my mind, so I kept my mouth shut and only widened my eyes in an invitation to share more.

"It has come to my notice that several people have been buried in the cemetery with valuables still intact. Gold rings. Pearl necklaces. Even, in one case, a state-of-the-art computer." His flabbergasted expression conveyed both disgust and disbelief.

I was thoroughly confused. "Who cares? I mean, the computer isn't worth anything these days, and what people want to take to the grave is between them and their loved ones, right?"

Jake's smile offered condolences on my ignorance.

He stepped closer and took my arm in a confiding manner. "These times, as you call them, are merely temporary. Technology has not been erased, just arrested. Once it is loosed again, then those who have made the most of the circumstances will prove their true worth. The next world leaders—if you understand my meaning."

Suddenly, cold shivers ran over my body. I understood him all too well. "If you're suggesting that I sink to grave robbing to get rich in some future reality, then you have another thing coming!"

A snorted laugh told me what to do with my comment. Jake eyed me with a sad shake of the head. "Nothing of the sort. You've got nothing to worry about, Rosie. I have plenty of assistants who take care of my business. I simply ask that you focus on what you're good at—and not worry about what isn't your concern."

The hint of a threat in his tone warned me to watch my next words. "I keep a close eye on the cemetery—it's entrusted into my care by the community. Nothing has changed so far as I can see."

Jake peered into my eyes—a mesmerizing experience. "There's a new world order rising, Rosie. Technology was halted for a very good reason. And it will recommence when we're ready. Don't forget that."

Even after Jake had passed over the threshold and out the kitchen door, I felt a coldness that I'd never experienced before.

Ben stepped into the room, set the empty bucket aside, and wrapped his arm around my shaking shoulders. "He's the devil's minion, all right."

I had to agree.

Chapter Twenty-Six

Humiens

October behaved itself, for the most part, right up until the middle of the month, when the night temps dipped into the low forties. Then push came to shove, and I had to either start heating the house or freeze to death.

Mid-morning on a cloudy Wednesday, I tugged my worn jean jacket over the thickest sweater I owned, slipped my feet into hiking boots, and tromped into the crisp air. My mission? Gather a pile of windblown sticks before the bunching clouds, and their soaking rain made every burnable branch completely useless. The red and gold leaves swirled to the ground, making a gorgeous background, and the slow exercise did me a mountain of good.

Mesmerized by the serene atmosphere and near Zen-like state of being, a gurgled throat-clearing jerked me out of my reverie. I turned with a load of broken branches in my arms and took in the startling scene.

Mrs. Bolder stood next to the old wooden swing set, clearly in no mood to play games. Her scowl seemed to set the leaves to falling like hand grenades. She thrust her hands on her hips and made her declaration. "My grave's been robbed—pillaged really—and I want justice."

First things first. I strode over to the overhang where the wood stack looked like something out of *Country Living* and dropped my load. Rubbing my back, I stared at the buxom woman. "How's that again?"

A frustrated hippopotamus squelching out of a muddy river could not have appeared more disgruntled. "I went by the cemetery with a bouquet of autumn leaves—my son always favored their pretty colors. He was only fourteen when he passed, and I never forget to lay a few of the best before his tombstone. I was shocked to see the ground disturbed—dug up all around his stone. Now it's a complete mess of overturned grass heaps and dirt everywhere." Tears gleamed in her eyes. "Damn diggers didn't even have the decency to wipe the stone clean after their thieving."

My mind tumbled with outlandish thoughts, and I spoke without meaning to vocalize my conjectures. "Jake said something about people being buried in the cemetery with valuables still intact. But surely, he didn't mean that anyone should..." I swallowed back bile.

Mrs. Bolder's naturally pale face turned an unfortunate shade of purple. Apoplexy was next.

"Jake Uri? That scheming, good-for-nothing, I'd-trade-in-grandma's-gold-teeth-for-a-buck, Jake?"

Terror struck me stone stiff. Honestly, I didn't know what she'd do. I glanced around, half afraid that Jake would be summoned at the sound of his name. But, no, only Juan lumbered out of the house and jumped down the porch steps like the kid he was. He started to wave, glanced at the tower of rage before me, and then dropped his hand. A frown rose between his eyes as he plodded forward. "You saw it then?"

I thought he was talking to me, but Mrs. Bolder snorted. "You bet your life I saw it. And Tommy's grave wasn't the only one desecrated."

I grabbed Mrs. Bolder's arm. "How many graves were disturbed?"

Juan shook his head, his gaze sweeping the ground. "About fifty." He shrugged. Someone must've worked fast. That's a lot of digging in one night. I can't think how it was done without anyone waking up and seeing it."

I slapped my dirty hands on my head and plunked

down on an old tree trunk set by the woodpile. "But why? I mean, Tommy was only a boy. He didn't have anything of any value, surely."

At the ensuing silence, I looked up and considered Mrs. Bolder's stubborn glare.

With her hands clenched and her shoulders squared, Mrs. Bolder shouted her words so half the county could hear her. "I buried his inheritance with him. He was supposed to grow up and run the farm. Well, he didn't get that chance, so I buried some gold and silver with him. The whole place goes to charity after my husband and I pass. Nothing mattered but doing right by our son. He always did right by us, and I wasn't going to let death have the last word."

Cold seeped through me as it had when Jake mentioned the new world order rising. This was not rising. This was descending. At an alarming rate. Right down to the pits of hell. Graverobbers stealing from young boys and their grieving mothers? How could this happen?

"Well, I know who I need to see next." Mrs. Bolder sucked in a lungful, preparation for blowing dragon flames at Jake, no doubt.

"You can't go accusing him without proof. He'll laugh in your face." I didn't want this strong, determined woman humbled by the sneering visage of Jake Uri. The very thought of it snuffed out something decent and good that the world dearly needed.

Juan gestured with his chin toward the neighbor's house. "Sophia's visiting, and I think she'd like to know your thoughts on these events before we make a plan."

I breathed a sigh of relief, gratitude pouring from my whole being as I admired my dark-headed, clear-eyed son.

Without another word, Mrs. Bolder belied her name and tromped across the yard and down the road.

I patted Juan on the shoulder. "Thank you. I was afraid she'd find Jake and string him up all by herself before there was any proper investigation."

Deadpanned, Juan stared at me. "He should be strung up. He may not have done the digging, but he organized it. I know that for a fact. And so do a lot of other people. But he's untouchable, so he'll go on wreaking havoc wherever he wants and make fun of everyone too vulnerable to fight back."

I rose to my feet and stretched, new strength filling me. "But he won't go unchallenged. Together we're not vulnerable; we're strong. Ben, Sophia, our neighbors, and the whole town will rise up and support Mrs. Bolder." I scowled at the name. "What's her first name anyway? I'm always afraid I'll get mixed up and call her rock or stone or something."

"Patty."

Hardly what I expected, I shrugged. "Okay. I can remember that." Raindrops fell and splattered on my face and jacket. I grabbed an armload of sticks and nudged Juan to the house. "Help me get a couple of loads inside before the temps drop tonight. We'll need a good fire." At the happy image of a hot cup of tea before a crackling fire, a warm glow ignited inside me, displacing all the horror of the morning. "Jake may be a scheming, good-for-nothing, but at least there's not really a new world order in the works." I ran for the house.

Jake sprinted ahead and, adjusting his sticks in one arm, he opened the door for me. "Hate to tell you, Mom, but there is—known as Humiens. They're in charge now. And Jake works for them."

Aw, dang. Even a hot cup of tea and a good fire couldn't warm me now.

Chapter Twenty-Seven

Pick a Side?

"What are we going to do now, Mom?" Bundled in a warm blue pullover, Dana sat on the couch next to me in the living room. Our feet were propped on the same blue ottoman, and we both held hot cups of mint tea that sent wispy swirls into the cold night air.

Casual, as usual, Ben wore his typical flannel shirt and leaned back in an overstuffed chair with one jean-clad leg crossed over the other.

Juan, still in his lumberman coat, sat on a stool across the room and leaned forward, his hands clasped, a young man with an old man's concerns.

A knock on the door announced the expected visitors. Though I had little to offer in the way of refreshments, I did have a bowl of popcorn resting on the piano stool just in case someone got the munchies while discussing the possible extinction of the human race.

I opened the door, gratified to see Linda, Josh, and Sophia standing on the porch.

Okay, the world as we knew it had already ended, but important qualities held us together. Love and devotion still mattered.

Take that, New World Order!

I retrieved the kettle bubbling on the stovetop and poured steaming mint tea into three mugs. Bundles of drying herbs hung from strings along the walls, making the kitchen and living room look like a set from *Little House on the Prairie*, but I had no intention of going tealess or letting my meals become tasteless even during a world crisis.

Sofia, never one to make an obvious fashion statement, did have a knack for looking good. Bundled in a long tan sweater over well-used jeans with her feet tucked into thick socks and wearing clogs, she looked ready to handle the autumn chill that had descended with early sunset as she headed for the snack bowl.

Linda hobbled along, clutching her husband's arm and looking like she had aged six years in the last six months. Her long skirt, wrap-around shawl, and loose silky hair should've given her a youthful appearance, but the dark shadows under her eyes belied any efforts toward serene beauty. She looked like weak tea in a paper cup.

Josh, on the other hand, hadn't changed much from the muscled guy who moved in ten years ago. Once Linda's dad died and her mom moved away, she and Josh took over the family estate and made a pleasant mini-farm, growing things for the holidays, like Christmas trees in a back lot and pumpkins for the Halloween season. He loved to work outdoors and had been developing quite a clientele until this present madness took over.

Despite the seriousness of our meeting, the thought of pumpkin pie and a couple of jack-o-lanterns to enlighten the porch swirled through my brain. *How can I even be thinking about such silly nonsense at a time like this?* My chastised spirit took umbrage and snapped a quick response. *Somebody ought to remember what happiness looks like!*

"Mom?"

I glanced over.

Dana nudged me. "You never answered my question, and we'd all like to hear what you think." She smirked. "Where do you go in that head of yours?"

I glanced around. Ben now stood next to Josh, while Linda had taken my seat on the couch. Sophia munched contentedly from the popcorn bowl.

I laughed. "Why do you care what I think? I'm looking for answers just like everyone else." Why my words came out doubtful-like, I wasn't sure. But then it hit me. I did have *my* answers. I knew who I was and why I existed, so the whole crazy world could spin itself dizzy, and I would not care.

Ben tilted his head in the funny way he had and stared at me as if trying to classify a strange bird. "What were you thinking about just a moment ago—when you were smiling?"

In sudden need of popcorn, I joined Sophia at the feeding trough and grabbed a handful of kernels. "I was just thinking about the holidays and how happy they make me...and how I wasn't going to forget how to be happy." I glanced at Josh and just barely restrained myself from asking if he would let me pick out a few plump pumpkins for pies and jack-o-lantern. I munched instead.

Dana rolled her eyes. "You're not taking our situation seriously, Mom. These human-aliens, Humiens, have taken over the planet. We are now ruled by a triune—Sabba, Nos, Tirips. They decide our fate, and we have to pick a side. It's them or us."

My mouth had gone as dry as the Sahara Desert, so I had to choke down my crunchy snack. But my umbrage was back in full force. "So what? Do they think that they can rule a planet without farmers? Without doctors and nurses, teachers, builders, police, and mechanics? Do they have another population they want to plant here in our stead?" Horror chilled my skin at the thought. "Because if not, then they are at our mercy, really. What do we care if they say they rule the world? They can sit on their thrones like emperors of old, but it was always the peasants who got the work done anyway. And if we're going to be peasants, I say that we might as well be happy peasants and have some jack-o'-lanterns and pumpkin pie!"

Only Ben clapped—good man that he was. My children and neighbors stared at me as if I had grown horns. Sophia, to her credit, nodded agreeably and took another handful of popcorn.

Something about those names bugged me. I grabbed my cooled tea and took a long swig. *Oh, Lord in Heaven.* Suddenly everything became clear, and I understood. It was the end of the world. But not in the way they thought. Blind fools that we were, we never saw the obvious.

Chapter Twenty-Eight

Marked

I could feel the storm before it hit. I lay in bed feeling restless as the wind picked up. At first, I kept my eyes closed and simply scrunched the thick blanket closer around me. A thread of a dream perplexed my mind—something about traveling to a haunted house that turned out to be a church where Juan and Dana played hide and seek. The very weirdness of the vivid scenes running through my head unnerved me. Brilliant autumn leaves swirled outside the dream-world window while my grown kids acted like goofy tykes high on Halloween candy.

A distant shriek forced me upright with a jerk, sending my aching shoulders into fits. *No more carrying three logs at a time into the house.* The aftermath of a cat's yowl sent me to the edge of the bed, where I dropped my feet onto the floor. Gaining my land legs, I shakily peered through the bedroom window.

The big maple tree groaned, and the old pine tree swayed. Leaves swirled through the air, but they looked like off-kilter bats veering crazily in all directions. Unease filled me. November was nearly upon us. Just Halloween weekend to get through. Not that Halloween meant much to me personally. I was never as attached to it as the kids were. They planned to make autumn cookies on Friday, hand out homemade popcorn balls on Saturday, and enact scenes from spooky movies each evening. Ben even went so far as to trade some of our best pecans for a box of cocoa and a gallon of fresh milk.

The cat howled again. Perplexed, I shuffled to the kitchen and cracked open the back door. Spoiled beyond words, my cats expected to be fed and patted whenever I appeared in their territory, but they rarely picked fights or acted viciously. Rainstorms normally sent them huddling together in the barn.

A fine spray washed over me, chilling me to the bone. When a strange black shadow leaped up and scratched my arm, I was shocked beyond words. My animals occasionally laid out territorial markers, but they never got uppity with me. Never. Not until now.

Before the storm could drench my clothes any further, I shut the door, holding my injured arm and musing on which of my adorable animals had turned traitor. But I hadn't seen anything clearly. *Could've been a stray, a wild cat who didn't know any better.*

The sting directed me to the bathroom, where I lit a lantern and took a good look at the damage. A nasty gouge shaped like a ragged S. Confused by my weird dreams, unsettled by the storm, and hurt by the unjust attack, I dabbed a blend of antiseptic and purified water to clean the wound. Then I wrapped it in a gauze bandage. Tomorrow I'd have Ben or one of the kids look at it and see what they thought. I had little doubt that my arm would heal from the scratch. But that wasn't what bothered me. The whole event felt staged. As if I had been led from a bad dream to a troubling reality—and marked as a warning. *For what?* I couldn't say. But it felt horribly intentional. The name Sabba flashed in my mind

A streak of lightning zigzagged across the windowpanes.

Within seconds, thunder crashed, shaking the whole house in tempestuous anger.

I scrambled for bed, grabbed the covers, and ducked my head. *Oh, God, just get me to the morning.*

~~~

"Rosie?"
~~~

I heard the voice before I saw the face leaning down close to mine. My eyes felt heavy, and my whole body ached. Had I wrestled a bear during the night? Then I remembered a fragment of my wild dreams and the crazy cat business. I opened my eyes and pulled my arm free of the covers. I peeled back the bandage. Sure enough, there was the blazing red scratch. Apparently, I hadn't used enough antiseptic.

"Uh oh, that doesn't look too good." Crouched at my bedside, Ben lifted my arm and inspected the damage. He pressed the palm of his hand to my forehead. Then he stood up and bellowed, "Dana, get a basin of hot water, antiseptic, and a large glass of tea for your mom."

Juan trotted into the room, his booted feet thumping across the old wood floor. "What's wrong?"

Dana called from the distance, "Be there in a minute. There's a dead cat on the porch I need to dispose of—stinking mess!"

Ben cleared his throat as Juan edged closer. "Hey, Mom, you okay?"

I hated the worry icing his usual calm tone. I tried to sit up, but my head throbbed. Intending to reassure him that I was fine, some form of gibberish poured forth instead.

Ben and Juan retreated to the middle of the room. Ben dropped his voice to a whisper. "She's been marked."

No gasp. Just dead silence. *I* would've gasped had my lungs been in a cooperative mood, but I wouldn't have understood what I was gasping about. Just the idea of being "marked" and feeling like driftwood washed up on shore didn't incline me towards cheerful thoughts.

Dana tromped in, her voice much too loud. "What the H is going on around here? First that ruckus last night and then the messy remains of a cat scattered across the front porch. We'll have to barter for more dogs. That collie hi-tailed it to the barn and probably spent the night saying prayers of deliverance."

I didn't hear Dana step up, but I'd know her touch anywhere. A woman's touch, much softer than her tone. "Oh, Mom." She sounded mournful as if I were already at the pearly gates waiting for opening time.

I tried once again to shift my position, but even with my eyes closed, the entire universe spun, and wooziness rose in a warning from my middle. I lay still and prayed that if it was my time, the gates would open soon.

Chapter Twenty-Nine

Halloween Night

It's amazing how after being ill, just feeling normal was a cause for celebration. By Sunday afternoon, I could sit up without my head throbbing, and my body responded when I cajoled it out the bedroom door and into the kitchen.

Sophia sat at the table with a pie before her.

I blinked. "Sophia?"

With a wide-eyed grin, she shot up and reached out to assist me to the table.

I moved like an old lady, checking every second to make sure that I would land on the bench and not the floor. When had I become so feeble?

Sophia eyed me with the finesse of a well-practiced physician. "Your color is good, and your eyes are clear. Not wincing in pain. That's a relief."

I glanced at the pie and remembered that it had been days since I had last eaten. I rubbed my cheek and tried to think of a good way to transition our conversation from detailing my illness to "Let's eat the pie before the kids get here."

Sophia practically read my mind. She rose and grabbed a couple of plates and glasses from the cabinet. Then she went to work. I sat back and luxuriated in being waited on, watching her swift, competent motions as she cut the pie into generous pieces, poured milk into glasses, and arranged napkins with forks within easy reach. Life stirred in my limbs.

Within seconds, we both dug in.

Once satiated, I wiped my face clean and considered the kind, courageously intelligent woman before me. "So, what happened? Dumb luck that a wild cat came out of nowhere and scratched me?"

Sophia held my gaze, her eyes steady, penetrating. She managed to answer a question without saying a word.

I sighed. "Yeah. I know. It was intentional. But I don't get it. Who would send a deranged animal my direction?"

With a half-snort, half-grunt, Sophia leaned back, her gaze wandering to the window. "You weren't the only one attacked. Twenty-three people that I know of were in some kind of altercation with an animal that night." She shrugged. "I don't know if animals were poisoned on a massive scale or if there was some kind of demonic possession driving them mad, but in any case, a lot of people got hurt. Well over half of them have died."

Horror ripped through me, sending fresh chills down my spine. "Am I going to—?"

Sophia rose and stacked the empty plates. "Nope. You're one of the lucky ones. Those who died went from bad to worse pretty quickly. Infection went to their heart, lungs, or brain. They never stood a chance. Even had our hospitals been running at peak performance, I don't think we could've saved them. It was something we've never encountered before. A new evil manifestation, very powerful, very unpredictable."

My stomach clenched. "Can it happen again?"

"Any time. We just don't know what we're up against." Sophia sloshed water into the sink and swirled in a sprinkling of soap. "No, that's not true. Sabba, Nos, Tirips have made it clear that they will brook no opposition. Fear, chaos, and pain are the weapons of choice. Whether it's them or us causing it, I'm not sure."

I blinked back tears. My body rejoiced at the food coursing through my system, but my heart cringed at our shared future. "I don't understand. Who are these beings, these Humiens? Why do they hate us?"

Sophia set a kettle on the stovetop and added a few sticks to the fire. She glanced at the hanging herbs. "You mind?"

I shook my head. "Please. A cup of hot tea might take the chill off."

With that, Sophia dragged forth a chair, climbed up with the agility of a woman in her thirties rather than her sixties, and pulled a loop of dried mint leaves from a hanging strand. She got down and sucked in a deep breath as she smashed the dry leaves into a tea-ball. "They're aliens with distant human affiliation. At least, that's what they say about themselves. As far as I can determine, and I only know what Ben and other friends can ferret out from various communication lines, they have human DNA but just a touch. They are unfamiliar beings—not even like each other. In other words, they aren't one species. They are a mystery that we can't wrap our minds around. At least not yet." She poured hot water through the tea strainer, sending a glorious minty spell into the air.

I accepted the hot cup and took a tentative sip. It felt good to warm my hands and my insides.

Sophia sat on the bench beside me, leaning back on the table edge. She sipped and paused, as if considering how to best inform me of the latest madness to have taken over our world. "They've organized things so that each town is managed by an Overseer. A certain number of towns or cities are governed by a Planner. Planners get together and report to a Counsel. Counsels report to Stewards. And the Stewards stay in constant communication with the Triune. They have generously announced that we can continue to live as we have done for the time being, but their system must be respected, and when suggestions are made, they are to be taken seriously and implemented quickly."

The room spun with my effort to comprehend the

vastness of the new world order. "How can a mere three beings manage it all?"

Sophia tapped her fingers together. "Slowly and absolutely."

With no ready response, I sipped my tea and pondered her words.

The kitchen door opened with a rush of cold air.

Ben tromped in with Juan close on his heels. They grinned in boyish fashion as if they had been playing games instead of working.

Despite the dreadfulness of being sick and the horror of Sophia's news, I felt a naughty squiggle of impish humor rise inside of me. "You two have been playing football, haven't you? I bet the cow is waiting to be milked."

Ben offered a wry smile. "Old cow is fat and happy, and Dana sent tonight's milk to the Henderson's. If your son here challenged me to a race across the yard, well, I couldn't let the boy down, now, could I?"

Charging across the room, Juan didn't make any comment as he eyed the pie. "This is supper, right?"

Sophia pointed to the dark refrigerator. "I put a pile of ham sandwiches in there for you. The pie is just a conversation starter." She rose and carried her empty cup to the sink. "I tried to explain how things are, who's in charge and all."

Juan snorted as he cut a piece of pie, dug it out with a fork, and balanced it on the palm of his hand. His eyes never left the crispy apple goodness. "They may be in charge of the world, but I'm still in charge of me. Pie and I were made for each other."

Grinning, Ben clapped Juan on the shoulder then grabbed himself a slice.

Sophia winked at me, and my heart relaxed. It may be Halloween night, but I might make it to All Saint's Day after all.

Chapter Thirty

Relationship?

By the 3rd of November, I stood in the kitchen on a cold morning, glad that All Saint's and All Soul's Days were behind us, and we could focus on Dana's birthday. She'd be twenty-three on the 4th, and by all rights, she should've been living in the big city, working at her chosen profession as a chemist in a medical laboratory, and having fun with new friends. Instead, she spent much of her day visiting neighbors and helping them manage difficult jobs: weather stripping old houses, bartering for needed goods, listening to complaints, and occasionally acting as a nurse by bandaging minor cuts and bruises. Early this morning, she and her brother had hurried out to help harvest the Livingston's back quarter of field corn. She wore her heavy coat and gloves while Juan sauntered out with merely a long sleeve plaid shirt hanging over his jeans and a pair of well-worn boots.

I waved to them through the window as they shuffled over the spray of falling leaves. Then I warmed a cup of tea on the stovetop and leaned on the counter as I considered my options. I didn't have the supplies for a lavish dinner, but I could make a delicious carrot cake—one of her favorites. Ben had carved a beautiful oak shelf for her room, so she could show off some of her latest treasures: a lavender plant that she had kept alive despite my dire predictions, a set of perfectly preserved arrowheads she'd found while repairing the foundation of an old barn, and a large dreamcatcher that an old woman presented to her two days before. Juan wouldn't tell us about his gift, but the twinkle in his eyes suggested something creative that we'd all enjoy.

Despite the NOW—New World Order—clouding the

horizon, my spirits were better than I expected. In truth, I marveled at myself. How could I feel any joy after so much bad had happened? Thoughts of Liam rambled through my brain as I greeted him and all the souls of my departed family and friends in prayer each morning.

"Good morning, Liam, Mom, Dad, Auntie Jane, Edward..." The list was getting longer as the town's folk passed away. I tried to keep up, but after a while, I just lumped the majority into one category "...and friends." Daily prayer helped to ease the grief of loss, but I couldn't explain my sense of calm in the face of such horrific uncertainty.

With a startling level of fickle-heartedness, I discovered that whenever Ben entered the room, my gaze lingered on his strong hands, broad shoulders, and disarming blue eyes. He didn't seem particularly disturbed holding my gaze, or my arm, as the case may be. What was wrong with us? Four months! Four bloody, horrific months, and we were cresting the edge of a new relationship. *Relationship?* I didn't know what to call it. Ben had slipped into my life as if destined to play his part in our struggle to find sanity in a mad world. Yet, I didn't really know him. Heck, I could hardly define him. Some kind of Humien—an alien from another planet, with similar DNA—who grew up on Earth was hardly a compatible match. I knew that opposites attracted, but this teetered on absurdity.

Yet my gaze lingered on him every chance it got, and my heart rested in absolute confidence. He was a good man, even if I was using the term "man" rather loosely. He was a good being? Different from simply being good.

I shook my head as footsteps padded into the kitchen.

Ben ambled in, rubbing his hands together, his

gaze on the woodstove. "You need some more kindling?"

I leaned over the wood box nestled between the chair and doorway. It was less than half full. "Well, I plan on baking a cake as well as some bread, so, yeah, that'd be helpful."

Ben rummaged in the cabinet and pulled out a plastic container of homemade granola. "You're making carrot cake, right?" He poured cereal into his hand and started to munch.

Flummoxed, I pointed an accusing finger. "What happened to your manners? You're reverting into a teenager." I slid a bowl across the counter and then slapped a spoon next to it. "There's milk in the cooler if you'd prefer not to choke down your breakfast."

Chuckling, Ben opened the box that we still used for cold storage, retrieved the container of milk, and assembled a bowl of cereal, adding a few dried blueberries with a flourish. He grinned at me. "Satisfied, *Mom*?"

I fought down a "go-to-your-room-till-you-can-behave-yourself" command and focused on the birthday cake. I waltzed around Ben, retrieved the carrots, eggs, and butter from cold storage, and then lined up the flour, salt, and baking powder. The bowls and spoons and measuring cups came next.

Ben leaned on the counter with his bowl in hand, eating slowly, methodically. He glanced aside. "Everyone has a season, you know."

Taken aback, I held the egg I had cracked on the edge of the bowl. The yolk dripped over my hand. "What?"

"We don't see the big picture. Not completely. All of this—" He waved his hand in a circular motion as if including the kitchen or the whole universe, I wasn't sure. "It's all part of something so big we can't see what's really happening. Liam did his part. You're doing yours. I'm trying to do mine."

My heart pounding, the crushed eggshell slipped through my fingers. With a muttered curse, I snatched out the shell and refocused on the recipe. I added a half cup of butter then furiously stirred it to fluff with a fork. "We aren't doing anything wrong. Is that what you mean? With Liam gone barely four months?"

Marching to the sink, Ben swished his bowl and spoon in the soapy water. "It's not wrong to recover." He laid the dishes in the drying rack and straightened, staring me in the eyes. "Whatever is true, whatever is noble, whatever is right, whatever is pure, whatever is lovely, whatever is admirable—if anything is excellent or praiseworthy—think about such things." He cleared his throat and shuffled to the door, grabbing a sack as he went. "Philippians 4:8."

Frantically stirring in the last ingredients, I wasn't sure if I would laugh or cry. But I realized, beyond any shadow of a doubt, I didn't want to face the future without that man.

Chapter Thirty-One

Chosen

Mid-November brought freezing temps, and fond memories of previous Thanksgivings with friends and family gathered for long weekends of fun and catching up. Just as dusk settled over the land, I swept old leaves, gnawed bones, and the remains of an unfortunate bird off the porch as Juan hung a pine garland that Dana had fashioned along the railing. His cheerful humming lightened my heart even as the vigorous cleaning stirred my blood.

Ever since the cat attack, I'd felt a strange foreboding, waiting for another charge from the enemy. Perhaps that's why I wasn't terribly surprised when Jake Uri climbed the steps and intercepted my broom's functional purpose.

The smile stretched across his face reminded me of an old *Mother Goose* poem.

Goosey, goosey, gander, where dost thou wander?
Upstairs and downstairs and in my lady's chamber;
There I met an old man
that wouldn't say his prayers,
I took him by his hind legs
and threw him downstairs.

The look on Juan's face suggested that he wouldn't mind tossing Jake across the yard. Since the garland was hanging straight, Juan had no reason to torment himself with Jake's close proximity. I gestured to the backyard. "Hey, honey, would you get some kindling to last through the night? I used up the last sticks making dinner."

Glaring at Jake, Juan's expression promised a future encounter before he pounded down the steps and into the yard. He snatched a wicker basket off the picnic table and proceeded to his duty. His long black hair rippled in a sudden breeze.

I turned and faced my opponent. "Jake?"

With his hands encased in fine leather gloves and wearing a long cashmere coat, the man didn't seem the slightest put out by the cold. His smile should have helped to warm his appearance, but it seemed colder than the dusting of snow we'd had the week before. "I've been sent with happy tidings, my friend."

A rumble, like the first signs of a kettle about to boil, bubbled from my depths. "We aren't friends, Jake. Not since you pillaged my cemetery. I know you had something to do with that!"

The look of absolute horror widening Jake's eyes gripped my heart even as I squeezed the life out of my broom handle.

"I had nothing to do with that. Nothing whatsoever. I swear to God!" With a fist pressed against his chest, Jake eyed me with an unflinching gaze.

Flabbergasted, my harsh judgments crumpled to the ground and scattered along with the dead leaves. "You didn't?"

"Why would I? I've been given a heavy responsibility as a Planner. I've no interest in pathetic little gains from minor grave robbing. The Triune entrusted this community—among others—into my hands for future development. Destroying a cemetery would hardly make a good first impression, now, would it?"

I swallowed a lump in my throat. A ball of disgust didn't know which way to go. "You don't know who ravaged those graves, do you?"

"If I did, I'd see that justice was done." His gaze leveled on me. "Certain members of the community who gained by that desecration suffered from unexplainable animal attacks right before Halloween." He shrugged. "I don't think it will happen again."

Jolted by this connection, I blurted out my thoughts faster than I could censor them. "But I was attacked—and I certainly didn't gain from the grave robbings!"

A knowing look practically glowed from Jake's eyes. "Were you? Hmm. That gives me pause." He stroked his chin and glanced aside as if weighing a heavy decision. Suddenly, he snapped his head up. "No, it must've been a mistake. You only gain through a minor reputation boost by serving as cemetery steward." He smiled down, a benediction of kindness pouring from him. "I'm still going to pass along their request—an honor, really."

Baffled by the switchbacks in this conversation, I leaned my broom against the wall and plunked down on an old wooden rocking chair. The sun had set before Jake arrived, and night was settling across the land, making the tree line across the field look like black fingers reaching for the last glowing embers in the sky. "What are you talking about, Jake?" Tiredness enveloped me.

Jake stepped forward and laid his gloved hand on my shoulder. It felt oppressively heavy.

"You have been chosen as an Overseer. The Triune has heard of you, and they are impressed. They do nothing without intention, and whenever they choose an Overseer, they allow room to rise and become more. Much more."

Shocked to the core, I jumped to my feet, nearly throwing Jake off balance. "What? Me, an Overseer? I can hardly manage my own home. Ben and Sophia do more overseeing than I do. Even the kids help out the townsfolk better than anything I could manage. Don't be ridiculous, Jake. Whoever suggested such an appointment to the Triune was mistaken."

Jake leaned in, his eyes narrowing. "No one suggests anything to the Triune. You don't understand, do you? They aren't humans. They can move at will, go any place on the globe that they want in an instant. They can appear visible or invisible, see, and hear everything. They chose *you* because they believe that you have the makings of greatness, a leader who can help not just a small town but humanity on a grand scale." He wrinkled his nose as if a disagreeable smell accosted his senses. "Are you going to tell them that you have no desire to serve?"

Pounding that began at the back of my head ran around to the front and played drums on my temple. I needed to think, but Jake wasn't making that possible.

Juan took the steps two at a time and tossed the basket full of sticks beside the door. He glanced from Jake to me. "What's wrong, Mom?"

I swallowed back rising bile and shuffled to the door. "I've been honored. Just not sure what I'm going to do about it."

Juan crossed his arms and glared at Jake. "You want to explain what's going on?"

Jake meandered to the steps. "Your mother is a remarkable woman who has impressed the most powerful beings on Earth. All she has to do is agree that they know what they are doing, and all will be well." With a chuckle and an impromptu salute, Jake bounded down the steps, whistling a merry tune.

My legs felt like water, and my whole body shook. I might as well have been standing on the pinnacle of a high mountain, trying to keep my feet against a gale wind.

Juan grabbed my arm, his voice tight with strain. "Mom?"

I shook my head, ironic laughter trying to force its way to the surface. "I've always been afraid of heights. Guess the Humiens didn't know that, eh?"

Chapter Thirty-Two

I Have My Own Mind

I didn't sleep well that night, and though the next day dawned bright and sunny with temps rising into the sixties, I felt more unsettled than ever.

Ben and the kids had gone for the day to deal with a mini-crisis involving three lost milk cows. Had the animals been stolen, or did they simply wander over a broken fence line? Since we no longer had hot wires to keep cattle enclosed on pastures, there had been a lot of missing animals and no end of disagreements. But with Dana's logical mind, Juan's natural charm, and Ben's good sense, I had no fear that they'd find the wandering quadrupeds and put things right before the sun set.

I should have felt as bright as the day, but I wasn't sure what to do about Jake's offer. Or rather the Triune's offer. I'd refused to have anything to do with their New World Order, but apprehension niggled at the back of my mind.

After a simple breakfast of tea and toast, I settled at the kitchen table and cut worms out of a pile of bad apples, then I dropped the apple pieces into a bucket beside a borrowed cider press. Apple cider was a treat under any condition, and this would make great use of otherwise useless fruit. Picturing myself sitting across from Laura Ingalls Wilder, I figured that I could hold my head up with dignity. She may have lived from wagon trains to airplanes, but I was making the same journey, only in reverse. My lips moved in my imaginary conversation though it was only in my head.

This is a whole lot harder, let me tell you, honey! You've never driven a car at 70 mph on a crazy freeway, had to keep up with social media, and managed the hundred and one techno-gadgets that kept our world going, then lost them all in one pitiful day, while still having to keep the home fires burning. And to beat all, I even get chosen as an Overseer by a race of aliens!

Oops! I sliced my finger. Flummoxed by my carelessness, I grabbed my hand and trotted over to the sink, where I kept a spare jug of clean water. I rinsed my wound and bound my bleeding appendage with a clean dish rag. *Stupid. I practically never cut myself.* With the resigned air of a doomed martyr, I arranged myself at the table and reached for the paring knife.

It wasn't on the table where I was sure I'd left it. I searched all around. Inside the apple bucket, on the floor, at the sink... I could not find that darn thing anywhere. With a heavy sigh, I pulled open the drawer, looking for the short-bladed knife that would serve just as well.

There was my paring knife. Clean as a whistle.

A shudder ran over my arms.

It simply was not possible that I had cleaned and put away the paring knife and forgotten I'd done it within five minutes. *Something* was going on.

I glanced around the room. What had Jake said about the Triune? *They can appear visible or invisible, see, and hear everything.*

I tried to remember if I had muttered any of my musings out loud. A hot blush worked up my cheeks, and I snatched up the paring knife with annoyance. "You can't intimidate me, you know. I have my own mind." I cut into an old apple and a fat worm squiggled in a desperate attempt to avoid being dislodged from its pleasant home. Mercilessly, I plucked it out and tossed its mangled body into the scrap box.

Overseer, eh? I swallowed. It didn't sound too terrible. I pictured doing the rounds of the neighborhood, checking in on families, giving advice, making reports, congratulating those who were doing well and—

"Hey, Mom?"

I glanced up.

Dana huffed just in the doorway, her red cheeks and bright eyes attested to a recent run.

"Yeah, honey. You need something?"

"You have an old notebook I could use?"

I frowned. "A notebook?" I rose and traipsed to my work desk, where I kept odds and ends. I pulled a half-used red notebook from a pile of old papers and handed it over with a ballpoint pen. "What's it for? You going to draw the cows a map so they can find their own way home?"

With a snort, she tucked the pen in her jacket pocket and slid the notebook under her arm. "There've been some disagreements about who some of the cows belong to, so Ben and Juan are going to survey all the ones in our area, numbers and descriptions, and the location of the pastures and such. This way, we'll have a public record and keep it posted here so anyone can check the facts. That ol' Riley fellow by Hurricane Creek insisted that Livingston's white-foot cow was his. But Ben remembered helping get her settled on the Livingston's farm, so Riley is having a fit. I think we'll have to come up with a way to deal with malcontents and shysters who're trying to take advantage of things." She winked at me. "Guess that'll be your job, eh, Overseer?"

My pride zigzagged to the floor like a slow-leaking balloon. *Oh, great. I'll get out a ruler and smack the ne'er-do-well over the knuckles for bad behavior.* "Thanks for the support, kiddo."

Dana chuckled herself right out the door.

With dragging steps and a throbbing finger, I returned to the table and my messy job.

I blinked.

All the apples were cut and ready for the press.

Fear raced over me. My thoughts about showing up Laura Ingalls Wilder seemed as ridiculous as a toddler insisting that she could drive the family car. The Overseer has an Overseer. *Always the way of it.*

I plunked down at the table and bowed my head.

Chapter Thirty-Three

Dream Comforter

I woke up late on Monday, luxuriating in a strange dream where a man with strong arms and the hint of a beard cuddled up close and held me in a gentle embrace. I had felt so safe, peace enveloping me, that it was like slaking a terrible thirst with cold water.

"Hey, Mom?"

Dana called from the kitchen.

"I'm coming, honey. Be there in a sec." A blatant lie, but we both knew what I meant.

I blinked at the light streaming through the window. Yes, I was behind my usual time, and I'd need to hurry to get the stove heated and breakfast ready for my hardworking crew.

Sophia and Ben were helping Dana and Juan on the town cattle survey—it was going to be a big project and involved "cooperatives," whatever that meant. Leave it to Sophia to come up with another way to unite the townsfolk.

I threw back my covers and padded across the cold floor, muttering in the chilly air. "Who is Sophia anyway? Isn't she a full-blooded alien or some such thing? So, why isn't she being chosen as Overseer?"

Unable to answer any of my whiny deliberations, I tugged on my jeans and an oversized sweater and struggled with thick socks catching on my chapped skin. Once I got everything situated, I huffed in annoyance and rammed my feet into my clogs as visions of lizard skin danced in my head. *I'll ask Dana about some lotion.* A tingle worked over my body as my dream flashed into my mind. *Stop it. You're a grown woman. In a crazy falling-apart world. Full of aliens. Humiens. Whatever!*

Shoving a strange craving aside, I hurried

downstairs, greeted my hungry kids, and got straight to work.

Juan had stoked the stove until it was hot, and I grabbed pancake mix I had set aside in a jar. I just had to heat the skillet, add water to the mix, and pour the batter. Before the sun had risen much further, Dana finished laying the table and arranged butter and jam in the center.

Loud laughter emanating from the kitchen porch turned my attention from my all-important frying pan.

Ben, with a nicely trimmed beard, shoved open the door, and a blushing Sophia scampered in ahead of him.

Startled, I watched them.

Sophia burst out laughing, one hand flying to her face, the other pressed against her heaving chest. She met my inquiring gaze, clearly amused but yet flustered. "Oh, Rosie, you're going to have to do something about this one! He's a scamp, and that's all there is to it."

A scamp? I blinked. "That's hardly the word I'd use. He's humorous at times and could charm the birds out of the trees, but..." What was I saying?

I blushed.

Dana sauntered up and slapped Ben on the arm as he washed his hands at the sink. "What you been up to, you ol' devil, you?"

The atmosphere suddenly plunged into moody blackness.

Ben snapped the towel off the rack and glared out the window, barely composing himself.

Sophia clapped her hands like a schoolmarm bringing the class back to good humor. "That silly man dared me to race him to the house. And like an idiot, I couldn't refuse."

Juan snorted. "At least you beat him. That's all that matters." He turned and offered me a meaningful stare, letting me know that he was hungry enough to eat everything in the house—*immediately.*

I flipped a couple pancakes onto his plate and told him to get started. Then I worked on refilling the skillet and told everyone to sit and that there'd be plenty in a minute. It took about half an hour, but soon everyone was full of homemade pancakes and jam.

Throughout breakfast, I watched Ben. He kept a smile plastered on his face, but the clench in his jaw suggested anything but happiness.

As they filed out the door, I glanced at my red, chapped hands and grabbed Dana by the arm. "Hey, you have anything I can use?" I lifted my red hands. "My skin's so chapped, lizards are looking down their noses at me."

With a quick nod, she turned and hurried upstairs. In a moment, she was back with a small purple jar. "I played around with an herbal-aloe cream mixed with oil, and it seems to do the trick. Smells nice too." She offered a sympathetic smile that I couldn't read and handed it over. "Use it all over after you wash up tonight, and it'll soak into your skin better."

Off she went out the door and down the steps, racing after Juan, Ben, and Sophia.

I stood on the porch and watched them traipse away, a strange loneliness enveloping me. Juan and Dana marched in the lead, while Ben and Sophia followed a distant second, their shoulders nearly touching as Ben tilted his head to listen to something Sophia was saying.

Who were those two? I knew so little about them, yet I needed them more than I had needed anyone—except Liam—in my adult life. And now, I didn't have Liam. Who did I have?

The happy group passed beyond the clump of pine trees and disappeared from my sight. I comforted myself with an obvious fact: *Dana and Juan are mine forever.* That was enough, wasn't it? Sophia and Ben didn't have to be my friends. I glanced at the neighbor's place down the road. Linda had grown distant as she became more involved with community matters and helping Josh run their growing farm. No fault or failing on either of our parts. Just the way things went sometimes. Close for a while and then...not so much.

Something inside ached as my gaze swerved back to the pine trees, and my dream comforter called to my soul.

Chapter Thirty-Four

A Moment of Weakness

The kitchen hummed with celebratory anticipation the day before Thanksgiving. Somehow Dana had rigged up a system to crack black walnuts without making a huge mess and staining the floor. It had something to do with Juan's weights, a wooden crate, and a series of pullies and levers that Ben had found stored in one of the outbuildings. She planned an extra savory stuffing this year. My stomach growled in anticipation.

Juan was working with some guy at the edge of town who had managed to raise a flock of turkeys despite the shortage of feed. They might be a little small and on the wild side, but being desperate to keep family traditions alive, Juan had arranged to help the man for a few days before the big holiday, earning a free bird in the process.

I cut up the last of the pumpkins with visions of pumpkin pies dancing in my head.

Ben had seemed more reclusive than normal, gone a lot, and hardly speaking at meals. I wondered if perhaps he was sick and didn't want to tell me. But this particular morning, he had jogged into the kitchen grinning from ear to ear, almost as if he thought it was Christmas instead of Thanksgiving, and expected Santa's gifts under the tree.

Around noon, I stood at the sink peeling potatoes for the potato soup I had planned for dinner. My face heated when he came in, as it was doing way too often these days. Something about that beard of his. It was mostly gray, but for some reason, my heart flip-flopped every time I saw it.

He brushed behind me, really brushed my back, leaning over my shoulder to get a look at what I was doing, though he could have seen easier by leaning from the side.

My whole body reacted in a way that I couldn't possibly manage comfortably. I scooted out of my seat, grabbed a glass from the cupboard, and poured myself a drink of frigid water. I poured it down my throat, wiped my face, and stared at the man smiling at me. "What's so funny?"

His eyebrows danced. "Not funny. Just relieved of a heavy burden. That's all."

Surprised, I peered at him, narrowing my eyes. "You get pardoned by the governor or something?"

He scratched his beard, a smile wavering on his lips. "Remember when Dana joked that I was an ol' devil?"

"And you got all huffy—though you pretended you weren't?"

"Yeah. Well, there was a reason. I'd been informed that Sophia and I had been chosen as Counselors. For different parts of the country, naturally."

My stomach dropped to the ground. "What? You can't leave! Sophia makes great plans and all; she can move around and serve anywhere. But you—you belong here."

Ben nodded, his gaze fixed on me. "That's what I told them, and, thank God, they agreed."

My body heated, and I clenched my hands together to get them to stop trembling.

Ben moved in, slowly and with perfect finesse.

I hardly knew what happened next.

~~~

As I lay in bed stroking Ben's wavy black hair, his gaze fixed on the ceiling, I knew exactly what had happened. Pure pleasure seeped through my pores. I hadn't felt this good in so long, I could hardly
~~~

remember when.

Ben sat up with a groan, a mutter slipping between his lips. “I’m not young anymore.”

Hardly the words of endearment I expected. Or needed.

Out the window, a bird flew across the sky, a speck before a pink strip of a cloud, warning me that evening was upon us and—

I jolted out of bed and dressed as fast as my fumbling fingers would allow. “I’ve got to finish that potato soup before the kids get home.”

Ben nodded and reached for his clothes. Suddenly, he stopped and grabbed my arm. He pulled me close and peered into my eyes. “This wasn’t how it was supposed to go.” He shook his head. “I don’t know what got into me. I was so blessedly relieved to be able to stay...” He swallowed and choked on his next words.

Shame and horror filled me. No, this was not how anything supposed to go. I stared at the rumpled bed. A moment of weakness? Extreme need? Fleshly desire gone rampant?

Ben let my arm slip between his fingers as he snatched up his clothes. “I’ll head out for a bit. Tell Juan that I’ll meet him in the morning at the turkey farm.”

“You won’t eat dinner with us?”

Ben yanked on his pants and slipped on his shoes without socks. “I need time to think.”

A shiver of humiliation worked over my body, all pleasure crushed to a pulp. I nodded dumbly. Though it had hardly been made consciously, the choice had been mine as well as his. I wouldn’t plead innocence. Just bleed silently on the inside from a wound I could hardly name.

Chapter Thirty-Five

We Slothed All Day

Thanksgiving came and went in a flurry of activity with the arrival of three wayfarers in need of cheer and nourishment. Juan had procured the turkey as promised, Dana fixed side dishes, and I provided pumpkin pies. Ben brought the guests—an elderly man who was attempting to cross the state to get to his family and a mother and child who had fled from an abusive relationship.

I was so glad to see Ben stepping through the doorway on Thanksgiving morning, I wouldn't have cared if he brought the entire Mayflower crew.

I shoved our confusing interlude behind me and focused on family and new friends. My efforts to keep the house warm despite a surprise snowstorm, set the table with a traditional Thanksgiving dinner, and make everyone comfortable kept my mind off recent events and my attention focused on everything but Ben.

During that day and the ones that followed, Ben maintained his equilibrium serving strangers and making arrangements for the old man to travel in good company and placing the woman and child at a nearby farm where their presence would not only be allowed but welcomed.

On a gray morning, after seeing our temporary guests to their new destinations, I marked the last day of November on the calendar and remarked to Dana that we'd need to start thinking about Advent.

Dana just laughed as she swirled the dirty dishwater down the drain. "I'm sick of planning for the next big thing. I'm tired of work. It's been nothing but long hard roads, painful duty, troublesome conflicts, and personal sacrifice for way too long."

She wiggled her eyebrows, an invitation to an unnamed delight.

"What're you thinking?"

Dana snatched a towel off the rack, dried her hands, and bellowed, "*Thinking* nothing! I found a treasure trove of candy on a high shelf in the closet. Last year's Halloween caramels, chocolates, M&Ms, and more, forgotten and untouched. This afternoon, I'm gonna lie on the couch before a roaring fire, relax every muscle in my body, and eat sweets to my heart's content."

My psyche nodded in wholehearted agreement. *I so deserve this!* "I've hidden a gallon of cider in the attic. I can even break into the chips and pretzels I was saving for the holidays, and we can sample a bit of salty as well as sweet. A great combination if ever there was one."

Dana grinned in delight. "Let me get my chores done, and I'll meet you back here at noon."

I glanced out the window.

Dark clouds bundled in the west, threatening rain, but I could finish the wash, hang the clothes in the basement, and put a pot of stew on for dinner for Juan and Ben before our appointed meeting.

I stuck out my hand, and we shook on our appointed plan.

~~~

In idiocy gone rampant, I even added an element of danger to the scene by propping leftover wine, whiskey, and vodka bottles on the counter. Liam had liked to serve liquors to his business associates, so we had quite a variety. I'd never learned to like the stuff, but on this occasion, I was determined to escape fresh embarrassment over my interlude with
~~~

Ben, haunting memories of my dead husband, and the grasping fingers of the Triune.

Dana stretched herself out on the couch while I took the recliner, and we started in, savoring peanut butter bars, nibbling chocolate delights, crunching pretzel sticks, tossing back healthy swigs of each of the liquors in a game to determine which was the nastiest, and chomping on handfuls of potato chips to clear the palate.

When the sun hit the tree line, my stomach roiled like an early warning system.

Dana lurched to her feet and, using an empty bottle as a pointer, she motioned to the mess of wrappers, scattered crumbs, and spilled chips. "We're terrible—Mom. You, me. How many sins we break, you think?

My blurry mind tried helplessly to focus. *Break a sin?* I swiped my runny nose with my sleeve. "Gluttony. Suppose."

Dana shouted in triumph. "And sloth! Hell, we slothed all day."

Defensive, I jutted my chin. "Not all day." Smarting from the memory of Ben lying next to me, my face flamed. *Toss in lust.*

Laughing uproariously, Dana started dancing around the room. "Sin is fun, right?"

Before I could react, nausea boiled into my throat.

~~~

When night fell and as Ben and Juan ate dinner, Dana and I claimed matching stomach flus and took turns throwing up in the bathroom.

I crawled into bed, shaky and disheartened.

Ben stopped in the doorway. He stood in shadow, an uncertain man in an uncertain world. I wanted to wave him away—back to whatever planet he
~~~

originated from, but the thought of Dana feeling as terrible as I did and my screwed-up version of motherhood, choked my windpipe. I could hardly breathe. I lay there flat on my bed and stared into the darkness. *Dear God, forgive me.*

Ben stepped closer.

Tears streamed down my face.

He sat on the edge of the bed, clasped my hand, and we both cried in silence.

Chapter Thirty-Six

Confession

The next snowstorm hit hard and fast. With some kind of extrasensory perception, I knew in my bones that it had snowed during the night. I rose before dawn and peeked out the window. I couldn't see much, but the light of the quarter moon showed hilly mounds that used to be our front yard.

I sat on the edge of my bed, my cold feet on the frozen floorboards, and I bowed my head. Something had to change. And it had best be me.

Strangely rested after a restless night—I knew I had a decision to make. I also knew that I couldn't make it alone. Weakness had me in its grip as much the cold had ahold of my feet.

What the heck is wrong with you, woman? You used to be strong. So sure of yourself.

Days long gone.

Without any concrete decision, I found myself sliding to my knees. The icy floor did not welcome me. But I didn't care. I leaned against the bed and clasped my hands in prayer. It wasn't words that mattered then. It was a sensation that I was not alone, and someone, some being beyond my understanding, stood close. Not Ben. I would have stood up if it were Ben.

I couldn't remember the prayers my mom had taught me as a child. Nor the prayers I'd heard others say in religious settings. I knew the idea of prayer...about Our Father who art in Heaven...or something. But no formula would save me now. No recitations or learned skills. A memorized piece seemed on the verge of obscene.

I simply dropped my head and begged. *Dear, God. Oh, please, God, help me. I'm so sorry. Help me do better!* Like some country singer who couldn't get beyond the first refrain, I kept repeating those words in mumbled, desperate fashion for I don't know how long.

Then my leg cramped, and it hurt like the dickens. Forced to my feet, I felt oddly relieved. A child who had cried on mama's lap and been caressed into soothing peace.

I sucked in a bracing breath, grabbed my clothes, and yanked them on my body. Then I scurried downstairs, kindled the fire with a few sticks, and put a pot on to boil. Finally, I snatched up my overcoat and plowed outside to work up a healthy sweat.

By the time I had cleared the porch and the walkway, Linda gingerly stepped into the new day, gripping her metal shovel like a skinny warrior facing the Huns.

Not particularly in the mood to chat, I waved and continued working.

By the time we met up, Linda stepped closer and eyed my perfectly shoveled walkway. "You get up before the birds to do all that?"

I nodded.

She leaned on her shovel and pursed her lips. "So, you gonna tell me?"

Fear turned my blood to ice. "Tell what?"

"When you're leaving. I heard tell that you, Ben, and Sophia have been chosen for"—she made air quotes—"prominent positions by the Triune."

My weary body grew leaden. I couldn't do this—handle everything without someone I could trust. I swallowed back my humiliation. "Can we talk?"

Linda has the ability to speak without words. Her expression started with *What do you think we're doing*? And within seconds morphed into, *Sure, honey, I'm here for you.*

I glanced at my house. Ben and the kids would be stirring by now. Probably already had breakfast made. Tears threatened to freeze on my face.

Linda grabbed my arm and led me toward her house. "Josh can take a hint, so if we go in and I squint at him just right, he'll leave us alone. Okay?"

I nearly sobbed in relief.

It took the better part of two cups of tea and a heaping dish of scrambled eggs and toast to tell my woeful tale of sin and debauchery.

Linda munched and swigged. She was as calm in confession as any seasoned priest. Beyond a few wide-eyed expressions, she hardly said anything.

Once I ran out of words and wrung a kerchief into a wrinkled mess, I stopped and waited. For Linda. To offer advice. Or absolution.

She looked at me, sympathy pouring from her eyes. "You're a mess, honey. And I can't blame you."

I waited. For more.

She stood and carried dishes to the sink. Efficient housewife in action.

I sat and rubbed my tired eyes. "So, what am I going to do?"

Linda rolled up her sleeves and started mixing up a batch of dishwater. "Oh, I'm no good at giving advice." She plunged the dishes into the soapy liquid. "Besides, you know right well what you need to do."

I swallowed and leaned back on the chair, weariness and shame nailing me to the spot. "Yeah. I knew before, during, and after. But that didn't keep me out of trouble."

Expertly washing each dish and rising in turn, Linda stared out the window on the brilliant cold day. "I could tell you about how I slept with guys before I finally found Josh, and he nearly left me when he found out about my past, or about the smoking he used to do behind the barn like a stupid kid...or a whole bunch of our thoughtless antics that wore us down and made life hard." She shrugged. "But what good is my dirty laundry when you got enough of your own?"

I ran my fingers over my head, ready to pull my hair out by the roots. "Where does this leave me?"

Finally, Linda turned and faced me. "You got to admit that you're an idiot and can't handle life. Then go from there."

I slapped my forehead, anger seething. "Thanks, Linda. You're quite the counselor."

She shook her head. "I'm not, but Sophia has problems of her own, and Ben is part of your problem." She winced. "If we were kids, we'd go to church and confess our sins. Hope that God would forgive us...that stuff."

I stood, grabbed my coat, and strode to the door. What I didn't get in counsel and wisdom, fury handed me in abundance. With a stiffened spine, I nodded formally. "Thanks for breakfast and listening to my ridiculous recital."

Pity and sorrow colored her face. "I wish I could help. But I can't forgive you since it's not about me. I'm still grieving Edward. Josh works himself silly. We manage, but that's the best we can do. It's no wonder the Triune never picked us for anything." She sighed. "There's your bright spot. Maybe they'll leave you alone now, too."

The whole world could leave me alone as far as I was concerned. I tried not to slam the door as I returned to the great outdoors. Trudging over the wind-swept snow, which would have delighted my spirit at any other time, I pledged myself to silence. The world could go to hell. But from now on, I wouldn't follow along.

Chapter Thirty-Seven

Your Part to Play

Though it wasn't officially winter, it sure felt like it. Cold seeped into my bones and settled there when it wasn't blustering through the house. Each day dawned in grey eeriness. My joints ached as I stumbled from bed, tugged on my jeans and sweater, thick socks, and boots. Tromping downstairs, I kindled the fire like a sleepwalker waiting for the windows to brighten and my mood to lighten.

On an early Monday in December, I felt stingy and made oatmeal instead of pancakes. Neither Juan nor Dana seemed to care as they hurriedly sipped their steaming mint tea and slurped watered-down hot cereal.

Juan nudged Dana meaningfully as he rose from his place, his empty bowl a testimony to his ability to scarf down food. "They're probably waiting for us at the timberline. We'd better go."

Dana, chugging as fast as she could, finally bolted her last gulp of tea and shoved back her chair. She offered me an inquisitive scowl and then a peck on the cheek as she started for the kitchen door. "You're not still upset, are you?"

Pretending indifference, I shrugged in my best nonchalant attitude. "I'm fine. You?" I added a concerned mom-look for emphasis.

"Fine." Her eye's widened as she slapped her face. "Almost forgot. I promised some cider to make the day a bit more bearable. Ben's bringing a big pot, and we'll heat it up at the edge of the field—hot cider makes chopping wood more fun, eh?"

"But we don't have—" I cut my complaint short. We had enough. I guessed. Though it meant our supply wouldn't last through the winter. Maybe only till

Christmas. I slapped down my inner Scrooge.

Juan winked at me and dodged outside.

Dana retrieved two jugs of apple cider from the basement and hustled after him.

Such pleasant, hardworking kids. I had no right to gripe about my dwindling supplies. Heck, I had a lot to be grateful for. *Right?*

My head might reason, but my gut clenched like a shaking fist.

I cleaned up the kitchen, doing the same dishes I had done a million times before. Irritation flared with every repeated motion. Once the place looked decent, I opened the cupboard and found it bare.

Where's the bread I made yesterday?

I could name three possible culprits. Juan, Dana, or Ben had some noble reason for taking today's loaves. I wanted to crack their heads together.

Instead, I showed remarkable restraint and gathered the materials I needed for baking.

Gray, my decrepit cat, meandered in. I didn't have enough food to last far into the future, but I dang well was going to feed my pathetic feline. I reached behind the apple preserves and dragged out a dish of leftovers. Crouching low, I laid the dainty venison bits before the hungry animal. She practically bit my fingers off in her eagerness to scarf it down.

"You're welcome," I snarled as fiercely as any wild dog. Depressed, I plunked down and stared at the counter full of healthy ingredients, waiting to be made into bread...or muffins.

An old woman's voice rang in my head.

You are blessed. Remember that.

Startled, I leaped off the bench and whirled around.

No one.

A loud knock on the door just about sent me into cardiac arrest.

Frozen, I waited.

The knock repeated, insistent.

Gathering my wits, I scrambled for the door. I didn't care who was there. I just wanted to get something right today.

Sophia stood on the porch, a bright smile illuminating her face.

With a cleansing breath, I moved aside and ushered her in. The house wasn't exactly warm, but it was a sight more accommodating than the great outdoors. "Come on in. Get warm. I'm just about to whip up a batch of biscuits."

She stepped in, her cheeks pink from the biting wind. "That sounds wonderful." She rubbed her hands together.

I poured chamomile tea as she divested herself of two layers of outer clothing. "You certainly know how to dress for the weather."

With a shrug, she took a sip of hot tea. "I've certainly traveled far and wide. If that didn't teach me a thing or two, I don't know what will."

I measured ingredients, trying to think of something pleasant to say. A wall of discomfort had risen between me and the rest of humankind.

She leaned back on the bench and rested against the table. "I had a very constructive chat with the Triune, and you'll be glad to know that you've been relieved of your position. So, you don't have to worry about that, at least."

So many contradictory sensations pulsed through me; I couldn't think.

Sophia straightened, her level gaze, adding emphasis to her words. "They understand. You belong here, doing exactly what you've been doing."

As if I had been kicked off the high school debate club, I seethed with the unfairness of it all. "And what the H have I been doing? Perhaps I could have done some good as an Overseer. Now I'll never know, will I?" I hardly recognized my own voice. My hand itched to slap someone.

Taken aback, Sophia's eyes narrowed. "Ben told me...and Dana told me. Even Juan told me that you'd been having...issues. Look, Rosie, you're having a hard time—no wonder. The world's going through hell, our human population has dropped drastically, and this winter will be the worst in ages. Terrible suffering all around and no end in sight. You have your part to play. And it's here."

Shame flamed my cheeks. I plunked down on a stool, my fingers covered in sticky dough. "Doing what?"

"You're keeping your home alive. Your kids need you. The community needs your kids. We're all connected. I can traipse around and give reasonable advice and encouraging support. I never had a place in any particular family. The human race is my family."

My heart thudded. "And Ben?"

"He'll come with me. Neither of us really belong to anyone."

Tears flooded my eyes as a lump rose in my throat. *Not true.*

Undaunted, Sophia drained the last of her tea and stood. "Well, I can't stay. Wish I could; those muffins will be delicious, I dare say, but I have several more stops to make before the sun sets."

I didn't argue. No energy.

Surprisingly, Sophia offered me a gentle hug at the door. I imagined her traipsing along the country lanes with Ben, and I tried not to turn green with envy.

With a sigh, I closed the door after her and set to work.

It didn't take long to whip up a batch of muffins, so by noon, I had a basket packed with jam, muffins, and a dozen boiled eggs. I toted the luncheon to the edge of the field and followed the sounds of axes thwacking wood.

Ben, his jacket tossed to the side, split wood on one end of the cleared space, while Juan sawed a log propped on sawhorses, with Dana holding the wood steady. A few other guys worked on another wood stack, creating a scene of primitive industry. Smoke swirled from a black pot hung on a tripod over a small fire pit. *If only I could paint a picture of this.* Knowing my lack of drawing skills, I didn't linger on the thought. I shook my head in dissatisfaction. *This should be remembered—somehow.*

With his natural extrasensory perception, Ben glanced up and met my gaze. He smiled, a relieved look that spoke of kindness and appreciation.

My heart lurched. *Oh, please, don't leave me.*

Ben laid his ax aside and trotted over. "You want to try your hand at chopping wood?"

"I'd more likely chop off my hand." I lifted the basket and my voice. "Lunch is served."

That got everyone's attention. It wasn't long before the food was laid out, and Juan, Dana, Ben, and the two other guys were munching happily away. Ben poured me a cup of hot cider.

I accepted it gratefully. "This your cup? I can wait—"

He grinned. "Just drink up and get warm. You look half frozen."

I sipped, enjoying the sensation of hot spiciness spreading over my cold bones. I glanced at Ben. "Sophia came by." I wiped my runny nose with the back of my hand. "She told me. About you two." My voice dropped into a cavern. "Going. Away."

Ben stopped chewing his muffin and blinked. He looked me in the eye. "Yeah. I'm going—for a bit. Because it makes sense. I can report to the Triune and tell them what few other people can. They know about my history, and I've been investigating them." He leaned forward and dropped his voice. "Things are not what they seem. Besides, I'll be back."

Relief warred with hyper anxiety. “In a year or a century?”

Ben snorted. He waved at Dana, who stood with the two strangers, laughing. “Dana, come over here and tell your mom before I spill the beans.”

Sitting on a log by himself, Juan glanced over. He got up and followed Dana as she trotted across the cleared space.

She stopped in front of me, glancing from Juan to Ben and back to me. “Now, don’t freak out, but I’m going with Ben and Sophia—as your replacement.”

I slapped my forehead and nearly sobbed.

Juan patted my shoulder. “Don’t worry, Mom. I bet her that she couldn’t get the job done in less than three months.”

Dana laughed as she smacked Juan on the back. “You know how I like a challenge.”

Wavering between happiness and nausea, I stared into Ben’s eyes and, to my surprise—saw hope.

Chapter Thirty-Eight

I Tried

Jealously is a monster. I awoke the day after Ben and Dana had gone, imagining Sophia sauntering along with two of my favorite people in the world, laughing, stopping at farmhouses, townhouses, city homes, being invited in for meals, giving assistance, being regarded with all the favor of the Triune-Blessed and hoped that she would choke on a chicken bone and die horribly. Shrinking from my viciousness, I stomped downstairs and got to work.

Thank goodness, there was plenty of that to go around.

People were getting sick, and death smacked our world with a heavy hand.

By mid-week, I was so exhausted from a series of house calls that I wanted nothing more than to crawl into bed and sleep for a full day.

The sun had slipped behind the horizon when I flopped on the couch, ready to ignore the world for a century or so.

Juan stumbled in the door and bumped into furniture, muttering under his breath like a drunken sailor.

Not my problem. He can eat leftovers and go to bed. I'm not moving.

"Mom! Get in here!"

Juan never shouted. Well, except in fun. This was more a scream than a shout. And there wasn't an ounce of fun in it.

I scrambled from the couch, my joints aching, and raced into the kitchen.

Oh, God.

Leaning helplessly on Juan's shoulder was one of the guys who'd been helping to chop wood. Blood seeped around a bunched-up jacket pressed against his thigh. Looked like he'd cut his leg.

No time to be squeamish. I raced across the room, grabbed a kitchen towel, and pressed it over Juan's hand, applying as much pressure as I could, while Juan slipped his hand free and tried to maneuver the guy to the table.

Not being practiced in the art of first aid or making the kitchen table a triage center, we bumbled along, the poor guy slipping and falling a couple of times before we got him laid out.

Before long, I was a bloody mess, nearly matching Juan.

"Keep pressing down while I get some more bandages. We need to tie a tourniquet to keep him from bleeding out."

The guy groaned, his eyes wide, as he flailed one arm. "Tell Missy..." He gurgled and choked.

Juan pressed him back down, his own face a bloody grimace.

I tried my best to keep the man's bright red blood inside his body, but terror filled me as I recognized the throbbing pulse of his artery spurting rhythmically. "What the hell happened?"

Juan shook his head as he tried to tie a towel around the guy's thigh. "I tripped over him as I was walking home. I think he was cutting wood by himself—I couldn't see." Unable to get the towel to tie tightly, he smashed it against the wound, slapped my hand over it, and then ran out of the room.

Too horrified to cry out, I simply leaned with all my weight on the man's leg, as if trying to stop a volcano from exploding. My heart thudded against my chest, blind fear cutting off all coherent thought.

The man's head fell to the side, and he seemed to relax. All tension eased off. Shock mounted on top of shock. I screamed, "Juan!"

Juan raced in with a clothesline wrapped over his

arm. “I was trying to cut a piece, but the clippers were caked with mud. Damn it!” He unwound a section and started to wrap it around the man’s leg.

The man didn’t move or groan.

I stared at his chest. Still and silent. My hand slipped, and a pool of blood seeped across the table.

Juan kept wrapping, and then he tied the cord tight, pulling hard.

Nothing. Not even a jerk of discomfort.

I laid my head on the man’s chest. Not a sound. No motion.

Juan looked at me. He leaned over the man’s mouth, listening, watching.

Silence. The pulsing had stopped.

I lifted my hand, and the blood-soaked rag dripped, but the wound, a deep, wide cut, sat in a quiet pool of red.

Juan closed his eyes. Tears meandered down his face.

I sniffed and wiped my eyes with the back of my bloody hand.

Juan blinked and cleared his throat, resolution in action. “We’ll keep the cord tied on and clean him up, wash out the cut and see. Maybe…”

I knew it was useless. Death had caught us unprepared. Once again.

Though we stayed up the whole night and did what we could, acting as if the man were still alive to our kindly efforts, by morning, his stiff corpse demanded that we face reality.

I had hidden a sack of coffee away for a Christmas special, but I knew we needed something to get us through the day. I heated a pot of hot water and made the strongest brew I could manage.

Juan toasted two thick pieces of bread on the stovetop and then slathered them with honey. He handed me one as I nudged a steaming cup of coffee in his direction. We didn’t talk, sitting across from each other at the same kitchen table where a man had died hours earlier.

The toast scratched going down. I had to force my words out. "What was his name?"

"Chad. I think. Or Brad." Juan rubbed his bearded chin. "I didn't really know him. Tony brought him. Belongs in the next county—not married, just got a girlfriend, I think."

"Any kids?"

Juan shrugged. "Can't say."

"He mentioned Missy...that the girlfriend?"

"Suppose."

"Can you find Tony?"

Juan rose from the table and plodded to the sink. He placed his cup on the side. "I'll find him...or someone who knows." He peered at me through glazed eyes, flecks of blood on his face. He had changed his shirt, but his jeans were a mess.

"You'd better change before you go out."

He waved my comment off. "The way things are, I'll be digging graves in the next week or so. No point in messing up all my clothes." He grabbed his one good coat, stopped in the doorway, and looked over his shoulder.

"What?"

"You need to write this all down. Someday, we might forget, and that'd be a real shame."

I rose from the table, wiped a coffee drip off the counter, and remembered Ben, Sophia, and Dana traipsing over the hills and valleys. Off to see the Triune.

I couldn't save the man, but I'd tried. God, I'd tried.

I climbed the steps, dragged out the last of Liam's suits, and proceeded to dress the guy for his funeral.

Envy had not the least power over me now.

Chapter Thirty-Nine

I've Come to Believe

Rain. It pounded like fists on the window while the wind wailed. The natural world sobbed in grief.

I opened my eyes and saw only darkness. Once I threw back the covers, the glaze of slanting drops against the bedroom window framed an opaque view of the sleeping countryside. Bare tree limbs shivered toward a vaporous sky, and a few green patches in the yard contrasted sharply against the brown field across the road. Strangely, the red-berried bushes alongside the house undulated like fronds in a gentle sea, uninhibited it seemed, by the season's demand for starkness.

I stood in my warm pajamas and considered the majesty of the dull, colorless day. Drops hung in suspension on the edges of the outdoor furniture—metal chairs around a square table waiting for better days.

The image of a pen and paper rose in my mind, the kind used long ago before computers made typists of us all. I felt like writing—something. Anything. The desire felt urgent, demanding that I scour my closet before getting dressed.

Scour I did. Remarkably, I found a treasure trove of old notebooks and drawing pads I must've squirreled away long ago. Liam always had a thing for journal writing and amateur sketching—a very romantic image he carried about in his head, one he hoped the kids would adopt.

He wrote sentimental poems for me on Valentine's Day and adventure stories for the kids, which he'd read, acting out all the parts, at bedtime. Never helped to get them to sleep, in my estimation, but it sure helped to get them into bed, and that was half the battle. Happy memories washed over me. What a joy when Liam took charge—his brilliant imagination leading the way.

Where are those stories?

Various cleaning frenzies, where I had blindly tossed away whatever wasn't absolutely essential to human survival, flashed before my eyes. I cringed.

"Mom?"

Juan's voice, troubled and depressed, rose from the kitchen.

Oh, yeah. Hungry son. Survival and all that implies.

I scurried into my jeans, sweater, socks, and clogs and traipsed downstairs with a notebook and pencil tucked under my arm.

After breakfast, while the bread is baking...

It didn't take long to cook up a stack of pancakes and heat a pot of mint tea. We sat at the table, Juan eating methodically—a mouthful, slow chew, swallow, another mouthful, another slow chew...

I sat up, ripped a semblance of cheerfulness from my innards, and tossed off an attempt at normalcy. "So, what's your plan for today?"

Juan looked up, his skin as gray as the sky, his gaze inward. "Gonna do the rounds, check on the Anderson's and their cows. They haven't been able to get out of bed for a while. Plus a few others." He sighed. "Wish Ben and Dana were here."

I nodded. Complaints, like wishes, were as barren as the winter ground.

After clearing the dishes, Juan pecked my cheek with a gentle kiss, a habit that had developed out of nowhere, but one I appreciated with a mother's hungry heart. He slung his coat around his shoulders and rushed out the door, ready to battle nature and whatever other evils assailed him.

My chest squeezed in a painful grip.

Suck it up, Momma.

I finished the dishes, wiped my hands, stoked the

fire, and settled in the living room by the window. The rain misted in a fine drizzle, and light leeched into the room. I opened the notebook, clasped my pencil, and began writing—everything I could remember from the day Dana had left for St. Louis, Juan went camping with friends, and Liam prepped for his trip to Los Angeles. I hadn't gotten far when my hand cramped. I shook it, trying to circulate sluggish blood, when I heard the kitchen door creak open, shut with a click, and a heavy tread across the room.

I froze. *Juan back so soon? What now?*

I stood and waited for doom's heavy hand to strike again.

Dana stepped in. Her hair was matted, her clothes soaked, and her eyes red-rimmed.

"Oh, Lord, honey!" I rushed across the room. "What happened? You're a sight."

As thin and ragged as she'd looked the first time she returned, now her shoulders slumped in utter defeat.

"Sophia is dead. Murdered. I couldn't stop it."

In a stupor, horror held at arm's length, I heated a fresh batch of tea, chamomile this time, and stirred up a bowl of hot cereal. I had a venison stew planned for supper, but it wasn't nearly ready. I sat across from her at the kitchen table, double-checking the surface for any missed blood spots.

Dana slurped hungrily, her gaze down.

And Ben? Where is he? I ached to ask, but fear held my words in check.

Finally, Dana finished, shoved the bowl away as if disgusted, and leaned back, staring at the ceiling.

I glanced up.

Dana heaved a long sigh. "I never took God seriously, Mom. Never needed to. I had you."

Tears blurred my vision, but my daughter's eyes remained dry.

"Seen the devil himself, so I've come to believe."

I choked back a sob.

Dana scooted upright and dropped her hands on the table like heavy weights. “If Ben hadn't been there, they would've killed me too. Sheer hate—crazy violence that wanted nothing but to hurt and murder.”

Horrible images of mobs on television, real and fictional, flooded my mind. Bile rose in my throat. *Dear God, help me.* “What...happened?”

Her hands trembling, Dana clutched her cup and pressed it to her chest. “I wasn't anyone important, so they weren't after me. There've been lots of Overseers reporting to their respective Planners these days. No big deal. Most people can handle town counsels getting together for the sake of their neighborhoods. So, no one cared about that. And even Planners meeting with a Counsel didn't attract a lot of attention. Plus, there's been a lot of sickness, and everyone had been working hard to get the harvest in and food stored, so no one fussed about such stuff.”

My mind whirled, trying to understand where Dana was going. Too much back story. But then, Dana always did have a penchant for lecturing...

“It was when the Counsels started reporting to Stewards that people got nervous. And the Triune, in an act of complete idiocy, decided to make their first meeting with the Stewards a grand event. Well, then, all hell broke loose.” She closed her eyes and shook her head. “Literally.”

I rubbed my face, my nerves snapping. *Literally* is an overused device, often mistaken for emphasis when it just doesn't work that way. “Not literally.”

Dana's eyes snapped open, and I saw something I'd never imagined seeing in any of my children's faces—hatred. Pure unreasoned hatred.

“Yes. Literally! Hell. Broke. Loose. As in pure e-v-i-l!”

My mouth dropped open, wordless incomprehension.

With the nearest thing to a shriek I'd ever heard come from Dana's mouth, she swept to her feet and flung her arms in the air. "They weren't human beings anymore, Mom. They were possessed, doing horrible things." Pacing across the room, Dana's voice shook with agitation.

"Sophia kept meeting up with people, so we traveled together...first just another Planner...but then there were others, a couple of Planners...a Steward...then that idiot got the idea that we should all go together to the Triune—show them who they were dealing with. The whole 'human spectrum' he called us."

Marching back and forth across the room, Dana's gaze stared straight ahead, but it was clear that her mind was far from home.

"We headed to this mountainous thing in the distance; I've never seen anything like it. Between a medieval castle and a sci-fi spacecraft—enormous doesn't cover it. White in the main part but with green and blue towers...I can't describe it."

Shocked, I grabbed her arm as she passed. "You saw the Triune?"

Limp, Dana fell onto the bench by the table. "No. We never got inside. We were still some distance away. *They* were waiting." She shook her head, her eyes staring at the wall. "The Triune must have seen what was happening—how that mob of crazy people launched into us. Grabbing and hitting, swinging cudgels, swearing fit for the devil himself, kicking. I even saw one woman get..."

She dropped her head and covered her eyes; her shoulders heaved.

I grabbed a bucket.

Dana shoved it away and glared at me.

"They yanked Sophia from my grasp. We couldn't fight them. Ben did his best, but he's not superman.

Sophia screamed, but we couldn't get to her. Suddenly, Ben grabbed my arm and threw me over his shoulder. He butted his way through the crowd, *literally*, using my backside and his shoulder as a battering ram, and we made it to some dark, stinking out of the way place."

Dana squeezed her eyes shut, and tears spilled down her cheeks. "I passed out. When I came to, I was alone."

Stunned, I wrung my hands so tightly, my arms ached. "How did you make it home?"

Dana studied the ceiling again. "Strangest part, Mom." She dropped her gaze and locked on my eyes. "Remember, I never took God seriously? Well, once I saw evil up close and personal, I understood. The broken bodies, blood, a battlefield with no winners. I got on my knees then and there, and I prayed." She squinted. "Can't recall the words, exactly. I couldn't live with the evil I saw. So, I begged for help." She shrugged.

I squinted, trying to clarify the images in my mind. "What happened?"

"God answered."

Chapter Forty

Ready to Burst with Light Rays

The temperatures switch-backed like a trail up a mountainside. Freezing cold spitting snow one day, then a spike of unseasonably warm temps another. Grey skies matched my mood, so I sat in the kitchen on a particularly bitter day in the middle of the month, cracking nuts that Dana had collected.

Juan ambled in and nodded, his face sober but with a hint of determination in his eyes. He glanced at the stairs. "She up yet?"

"Nope." Despite slow-speed helpfulness, Dana had been sleeping in later and going to bed early. She trudged about the place like a rag doll with the stuffing kicked out of her.

Juan shook his head. "I thought she'd bounce back. That whole story about an angel leading her home." He tromped to the cabinet and dragged out a pot.

I frowned, my gaze following his every movement. "She's seen too much. We all have."

Juan snapped open the cupboard and grabbed a flask of oil and a bag of popcorn.

"What on earth are you doing?"

"Making popcorn."

"Now?"

Juan waved his arm. "Are there only certain popcorn days? When the moon is full, perhaps?"

Caught between hilarity and hysterics, I squeaked. Not a clear response, but all I could muster at the moment.

Juan smacked the pot onto the stovetop, poured in a huge dollop of oil, and then thrust in a handful of popcorn.

I shook my head, anger rising. "We don't have a lot of supplies, and popcorn is supposed to be for special occasions. Besides, oil is really hard to come by, and you just used a month's ration."

Juan scowled. "You're being ridiculous. Dana loves popcorn, and if it gets her sorry butt out of bed, it'll be worth all the oil we have—"

Pop!

Pop-pop

Pop-pop-pop-pop...

We both looked over.

Smack! Hit in the face with a white kernel.

I ducked as the popcorn projectiles shot all over the kitchen.

"Damn!" Juan raced to the cabinet, slapped things about.

As the popping produced a veritable storm, I shoved him aside, located the lid, and with one arm over my face, approached warily.

Juan grabbed the lid, used it as a shield, and then plopped it on the pot.

The cascade halted.

Relieved, I exhaled a long breath. Then I was surprised by a new sound. Laughter.

Dana stood by the kitchen table, laughing uproariously.

I glanced at Juan. He smiled.

Whatever it takes, God. Whatever it takes.

I spent the rest of the day working on my journal, writing everything I could remember from the early days, asking Juan and Dana to fill in the details, and eating popcorn by the handful. A blessed break from the deluge of grief that had drowned all joy in our lives.

Following my new rituals, I stoked up the fire for the night, then stopped in each of the kids' rooms and said goodnight. They now allowed me to give them a kiss and a hug before bed, something I never dreamed I'd get to enjoy again this side of the pearly gates.

I padded to my room and peeled my day clothes off, groaning at the thought of wash day. I just couldn't imagine scrubbing my clothes clean in this frigid weather. Thank Heaven Juan and Dana did their own, or I'd collapse at the mere thought of laundry. Shivering in the cold air, I tugged on my old PJs and pulled back my covers, ready for dreamland. An escape.

The steps creaked. Up, up, up.... Footsteps on the landing. Then across the hall, closer and closer...

Chills raced over my arms. I closed my eyes and backed into a dark corner. *No more, God. I can't take any more.* The steps halted. Crouching, I glanced up.

There on the opposite wall hung a picture Dana had painted as a child—a funny portrait of me with a glittery halo and light rays bursting from my eyes. I could hear her lisping little girl voice saying, "You make the whole house bright, Mama." I stared at my trembling hands. Is this how I want to face my end—cowering in my room? Leaving my kids to whatever fate?

I stood and glared at the door, my whole body trembling, but my heart ready to burst with light rays.

The door opened, and Ben stepped in.

~~~

We lay the rest of the night in each other's arms, and I didn't give a thought to temptation, the right order of things, rules, or the future. We were both so far spent in exhaustion that neither of us could have managed any physical activity more strenuous than a slow caress. I snuggled deep into his embrace, covered by three layers of blankets, warding off the night's frost.
~~~

His strong arms felt so good; I ignored the stink of sweat and filth that emanated from him. His shirt felt wet in spots, but I didn't care. I was so glad to have him back. Strength and hope incarnate. Questions rose to my lips, but I could not face the answers with darkness pressing against us.

I exhaled a long, relieved sigh and fell into a deep sleep.

Sometime during the night, a nightmare of swirling images crowded my mind: a flood of water rushing up the road toward our house, a mammoth tornado on the horizon, wolves clawing at the window. Dana and Juan were children again, cowering in the corner, crying, holding each other. But a ferocious beast slithered across the floor and opened its fanged mouth, ready to bite—

A shriek jerked me from my dream. I sat up, reaching wildly.

With hunched shoulders and bowed head, Ben rocked back and forth, sobbing.

I wrapped my arms around him and held tight.

After a moment, he shuddered and then stilled. He lifted his head and stared with glimmering eyes into my face. "I couldn't save her. I couldn't save anyone—except Dana. The damned beasts wouldn't stop. Oh, God! I hate the human race."

Chapter Forty-One

Why Do We Exist?

A break in the weather also brought breaks in two porch steps. Since their fingers wouldn't freeze in the above-normal temps, Ben and Juan took charge with manly ingenuity, a saw, thick slabs of wood, a hammer, and nails.

Dana set out for the hedgerows—she liked to gather kindling and haul it in, apparently constructing a Pteranodons' nest against the wood stack.

I stood on the gravel driveway and cheered the men on, pointing out that the hammer was best for pounding nails rather than fingers and other such helpful infomercials. I had a pack of band-aides stuffed in my coat pocket.

They measured, cut, and fit each piece in place. No words needed; they knew each other so well, a raised eyebrow or a head shake communicated their thoughts eloquently.

What is it with men and their complete disregard for idle chatter?

"You two could be father and son, the way you work together."

Before the words had disappeared into the air, I wished I could take them back again.

Ben's face creased into tight lines as he hammered the last nails into place. With a huff, Juan held the wood in place, then gathered the tools.

When will I ever learn?

What? My alter-interior ego asked plaintively.

To stop talking out of turn and say the wrong things, stupid-head.

Without a word, Juan shuffled to the outbuilding, carrying the tools and end pieces.

I stuffed my hands deeper into my pockets and

fingered the band-aides.

Ben rose to his feet, wincing.

"You okay?"

"Nothing that death won't cure."

I dropped my head onto my chest. Such a brief respite, and all was dark depression once again.

Ben wrapped his arm around me. "You did nothing wrong. Just so many bad memories. It's best just to concentrate on a job." He shrugged. "Any task will do."

I considered the sturdy-looking new steps. "You two do fine work. I'm mighty grateful."

After a half-smile accompanied by a bow, Ben reached for my hand. "Walk with me. I may not want to talk about it, but I think we need to face what happened together."

I clasped his hand and headed to the pine woods on the north end of our property line.

I'm not sure what compelled us to that section of the land, but after climbing over fallen trees and stepping across a shallow stream on strategically placed rocks, we found comfortable perches on a fallen oak tree. I sucked in a deep breath, savoring the glory of a winter woods. "It always feels magical here—like I expect to see fairy folk peek from behind a fern or splash across the creek bed."

Ben smiled, his eyes soft. Not a happy man, but no longer in agony. "The Triune isn't what you think, Rosie. They aren't the bad guys here."

Caught off guard, I jerked back a bit. "Aren't they? Didn't they cut off our technology, killing millions who needed food, medicine, treatment—How can you say they aren't bad? If they aren't, I'm terrified by what bad really looks like."

Ben clasped his hands together and peered through the foliage. "Sophia had met them before. So had I, and we discussed their true purpose. Though no one said it exactly, we both came to the same conclusion."

I lifted my hands in silent supplication.

"They were sent to test humanity. To see how we would handle losing power and pretense. Humiliation can make or break a person."

"So, all the death and destruction are our fault?" Fury boiled inside me, and the rising chill wind nipping at my nose only added to my irritation.

"It wasn't the Triune that attacked us. It was people. Men and women, even teens."

"They must've seen you and the rest as threats, right?"

"They didn't ask, and they wouldn't have listened even if we were given a chance to explain. Madness isn't reasonable." Ben rose and paced across the brambly wooded floor and faced an open field in the distance. The sun had dropped near the horizon, and slanting shadows speared the land.

"I got Dana to the safest place I could, and then I went back for Sophia. The crowd disbursed almost as fast as it rose—once our assembly had been scattered or killed, there wasn't much for them to do but move off and find another target, I suppose."

"I take it that you never found Sophia."

A tear meandered down Ben's cheek. "I found her. At least I found what was left—her body. Doesn't take technology to kill a person."

I closed my eyes, a tsunami of grief rising like a storm.

"There were a few strangers about, but I didn't trust anyone, so I carried her away and found a wooded glen. Took me into the night to dig a grave and get her buried properly. Then I just sat and wept. Like a kid, I couldn't make sense of anything. Why did my people return to this godforsaken place and leave me here? And how do humans, despite all their development, still manage to turn savage?"

I was sobbing so hard that I couldn't look up. Shame, remorse, guilt for the whole human race bowed my back till I was practically kneeling on the ground.

Ben's voice rumbled on. "Don't get me wrong, I know that there are good people. You, Dana, Juan, and lots of others have proven that. But you're also very weak. Put you under enough pressure, and you all break, in one way or another."

It was true, and I could hardly deny it considering my own wayward trends of late. What would I do if I were hungry, injured, or my children were threatened? I could blame, hate, and retaliate with the rest of them. *Why do we live, God? Why do we exist?*

I didn't hear an answer. But I did get a lift when Ben took my arm.

"Let's head back. Juan said something about bringing in a Christmas tree, and I don't want to disappoint him."

If I hadn't been so miserable, I might've smiled.

Chapter Forty-Two

Amen

The Christmas tree looked lovely in the living room corner with colored glass balls, family ornaments, and an angel wearing a long white dress perched on the tip-top.

Dana sorted the figures for the Christmas stable and even scattered some straw about to make it look more authentic.

Juan surprised us with hot cocoa that he'd managed to keep hidden away, making the evening a fun and delicious celebration.

Ben set the wise men and their camels in a long wandering line all the way across the room.

Dana laughed. "It's too late to put them that far away. Only a few days left. They'll never make it in time."

Juan squinted, a man measuring distances with his eyes. "No, they'll get there—they just need to cross the bookshelf, leap over the recliner, traipse across the living room floor, climb the cabinet, and squeeze into the stable."

Like bells ringing a familiar tune, the profound reality of Juan's words hit a deep chord, though I couldn't explain. I just nodded and smiled. "Leave them be, and let's see what happens, okay? Maybe camels, like reindeer, can fly..."

~~~

Traditions died hard in my world. In fact, they refused to give up the ghost, so once I started planning the Christmas menu, I then sent Juan out
~~~

to see if there were going to be any religious services in the area.

Liam had been raised Catholic but stopped going to Mass as a boy. I kept up the habit while the kids were young, but as time passed and life took over, I strayed like a kid who'd stopped eating healthy meals. Since I always returned for the big events—Holy Days, Baptisms, Confirmations, Marriages, and Funerals—sacraments all, I didn't *feel* the lack.

In the flurry of our changing world, personal devastations, transportation issues, and the fact that so many people suffered and died far from loved ones, religious services had dwindled to small, local events.

Logic dictated that I forget celebrating Christmas within a community celebration. Nevertheless, I only had two paths open to me: hope or despair.

I chose hope in the form of Christmas however I could celebrate it. And that meant baking cookies. And sharing them with neighbors. Heck, death haunted everyone—I might as well face the grim reaper with frosting on my lips and a warm feeling in my heart.

Mid-morning on that cold, cloudy Christmas Eve, I made up a tray of frosted delights, wrapped it in a clean cloth, tugged on my winter coat, and headed out to the Bolder's place. Memories of Chicken Day shot like fireworks through my brain. Patty Bolder may have been a force of nature, but she was also one of the best representations of humanity that I'd ever met. Images of her and her husband huddled close to their woodstove with herbs hanging from the rafters and not a cookie in sight hurried my steps.

Before I got halfway up the lane, three old hounds ambled my way, hallooing in the way only hound dogs can. I repeated, "Nice doggies, don't bite me," like a mantra till Patty smacked open the front door and grinned. She welcomed me inside with a rotating wave.

Bursting with my sugar surprise, I trotted forward at full speed and entered their warm house with the spirit of Christmas Present riding on my shoulder.

It was what I imagined but so much more.

The woodstove gave off a warm, comfy heat, while a loaf of nut bread snuggled on the warming rack. A pot of stew—venison?—gently bubbled on the top. Garlands of pine branches with pinecones and bunches of herbs and onions hung on pegs along the back wall.

A bowl of mixed nuts sat on the counter, along with two pies, loaves of bread, dried fruit, and what looked like huge pretzel sticks.

My mouth watered. Then I remembered my manners. "I brought you something—didn't know if you had any sweets for the holidays—and, well, here."

Patty grinned then bellowed into the next room. "Delmar, get yourself in here and see what Rosie brought us."

Delmar, grinning from ear to ear, ambled in like one of his rheumatic hound dogs. "How'ya, Rosie? Whatcha got there?"

With dramatic flourish, I whipped off the cloth and held out my tray of cookies.

To his everlasting credit, Delmar didn't even glance in the master-cook's direction. He just clapped his hands and beamed with joy. His red cheeks and bright eyes brought the image of a Merry Saint Nicolas to life.

Patty was a bit more practical. "Well, you just set those on the counter, and I'll heat us a nice cup of cider to celebrate. Take off your coat, and sit a spell. It'll be splendid to relax with company a bit."

After handing Delmar the largest cookie on the tray, I whisked off my coat and moved as directed to the living room. Dim, though still comfortably warm, the room glowed with soft lantern light. A Christmas tree stood in a corner bedecked with home ornaments and glazed popcorn balls. Red Christmas stocking with white trim hung from the upstairs balustrade.

It looked and smelled wonderful. A small manger set sat perched on a table against the back wall, and a stack of presents decorated the floor between the tree and the table. Quaint paintings and embroidery samplers hung on the walls.

I stared, trying to take in the charming details. An exquisitely painted birdhouse stood on a post in a corner, while hanging vines and ivies enlivened the walls.

Dazzled, I could hardly speak.

"You like crafty stuff?"

I focused my attention on Delmar, who dropped onto a rocker. He pointed to the matching chair and nodded. "She'll be in and out, won't want to sit but for a moment, so you make yourself comfortable."

I settled onto the padded chair and felt it sway backward. Such a relaxing sensation, the gentle back and forth. It'd been so long since I rocked the kids...

Delmar sniffed.

Embarrassed, I dragged myself back to the moment. "Oh, no, I mean, yes, I love crafts. Just don't have much time for them myself. Too busy with meals and housekeeping and such. You know how it is...you must be so busy running your farm."

Delmar chuckled as his gaze wandered the room. "Well, yes and no. I get busy at certain times of the year—calving, planting, harvesting. Like bees in springtime then. But Patty and I enjoy our evenings together. We take a little time to think upon a project, then gather the materials, then do a bit at a time, here and there—showing off what we've done as we go. Like glue with us, you might say. It holds us together, friendly-like, whether the day's been hot or the nights been cold, makes no difference when you've got something you're proud of to show to someone who cares."

Tears welled in my eyes. I learned more about marriage and friendship in those few minutes than I'd learned in the previous fifty years of my life.

Patty swooped in with a tray and bounded forward. "Hope you don't mind if we sample those cookies of yours with the cider. Seems as good a time as ever to enjoy a treat."

In a matter of seconds, I was enjoying myself like never before. The world and all its problems melted away. Patty and Delmar asked about the kids and discussed all the neighbors, describing nursing shifts they'd taken and regular donations they supplied to the food pantry. Surprised beyond words by their industry, I was even more shocked to discover that they still had fresh eggs.

"How'd you get them to lay so late in the season?"

Patty shrugged. "Birds are like children—treat them right, and they give more than they take."

I marveled.

Only when Delmar asked about Sophia did the joy die. I choked up reciting a quick version of events, but they seemed to read between the lines and understood the depth of the tragedy.

Delmar shook his head, his blue eyes watery and grieved.

Patty sat perched on the edge of an ottoman, clasped her hands, and bowed her head.

Suddenly she lifted her voice. "Oh, dear Lord, take into your arms our friend Sophia who did so much good on this Earth. We bear testimony to her gentle service, her steadfast charity, generous love, and great courage. Please, comfort those of us left behind, knowing that she suffers no longer but rejoices in what we have yet to understand. Amen."

Delmar's echoed "Amen" reminded me of a rock on the tempest ocean shore, smashed by waves for eons but remaining robust throughout.

My response was not just a prayer of supplication but one of immense gratitude.

Amen, dear God, Amen.

Chapter Forty-Three

I Once Was Lost

Cold seeped into my bones as the wind swirled through the cemetery. Vultures, hawks, and crows careened against the grey, threatening sky. Only a few mighty oaks rustled their leaves; the rest of the tree line swayed in eerie silence.

Linda and Josh held candles that could not stay lit in the smothering wind, but they didn't seem to care. Their mittened hands clutched the slim wax sticks like standard-bearers before an advancing army. Except we didn't have an army. We had common folk, weary beyond words and in no mood to fight.

Monument makers did their best, but there was no way to keep up with the current demand. So many had passed on that families took it upon themselves to fashion headstones, carved slabs of cement or rock, using whatever tools they could find—etching out names, dates, and a short quote or symbol.

My eyes stung as I swung my gaze from all the new graves and their fresh markers to Edward's tombstone, so lovingly created. Josh had spent weeks working on it.

Edward Nosrep
*19**-20***
Beloved Son

Linda's muffled sobs jostled with the fifty or so other choked expressions of grief pouring from the assembly—a community funeral to remember those who passed. There wasn't a dry eye present.

Juan and Dana stood at my side, while Ben

assisted Josh to keep Linda upright. I glanced around at the blurry vision of miserable humanity. Surely, we hadn't come to this—sobbing wrecks in a bleak, windswept cemetery with nothing to grab onto, no hope to lift us beyond despair?

Incongruously, a wavering woman's voice somewhere in the back began to hum. A hymn of some kind. I wasn't up on my Protestant brethren's top forty, but I recognized the tune. Then it hit me. *Amazing Grace.* Even *I* knew that one, though I couldn't recall the words exactly. More voices joined in the melody.

A man picked up the thread, his voice deep, haunting... *That saved a wretch like me...I once was lost, but now I'm found...*

I stumbled along like a sleepwalker, my voice joining theirs, a defiant shimmer of sound in the frigid December air, but the words made sense like they never had before. I wracked my brain, trying to remember the story of the song, how the lyrics came to be, and what they meant. But all that I could think about was this pathetic crowd, huddled together in one of the bleakest places on Earth during a barren winter evening, singing our hearts out. It was a triumph of sorts, though I couldn't understand why. The dead were still dead, and we still had to fight the elements to get home, struggle to survive, and wonder what it was all for.

The final words rolled over me, soothing my fears and healing my hurts, at least for a moment—*My God, my Savior has ransomed me...And like a flood, His mercy rains...Unending love, Amazing grace...*

~~~

Sleet started the minute the last prayers for the departed left our lips. It was a hurried mob that
~~~

charged against the icy onslaught, but Ben kept a firm grip on my hand and led me home. I was ever so grateful to slouch on the kitchen bench and allow Dana to scoop up the hot stew I had left simmering on the stovetop. I tugged off my wet coat as Juan added sticks to the fire, warming the chilly room. Ben cut bread and passed out the spoons. A family effort that resulted in a sustaining meal together. We weren't cheerful, but we were comforted, and after everything, I settled for that gratefully.

It was late by the time Juan and Dana wandered up to their rooms. I gave each of them a kiss and watched them ascend, so glad that they were a part of my life.

I looked over my shoulder.

Ben stood there, watching me.

Stay or follow the kids?

Ben plunked down at the end of the couch and patted the spot next to him. It had been ages since we were alone together in peaceful companionship. There was still something between us...yet a great deal never explained or understood. What did I want? *Beats me.*

Dragging my feet, metaphorically speaking, I meandered back to the couch and plopped down.

Ben tilted his head and gave me *the look*. The one that asked how I was doing, and if I was up for an honest exchange, all without uttering a word.

Being the eloquent one, I shrugged.

He wrapped his arm around my shoulder and drew me close. "It's been a hell of a time, but you know, we've been walking down this road a long while."

Confused, I scowled at my shoes.

"Humanity has been building one Tower of Babel after another—trying to reach Heaven. My kind wasn't much better. It's clear that we share some origin story—our DNA is a close match. Whatever happened to my people, they believed that humanity had something good to offer. Was it some rosy memory of an ancient home world or a fantasy plastered over reality? I don't know." He sighed. "But no matter, the fact is, they entrusted us into humanity's future."

I picked at a crumb embedded in my sweater. I was listening. Just didn't know what to say.

Ben nudged me, his smile wavering.

I looked up and met his gaze. "I love you." I shrugged like a bewildered kid. "I don't know about alien worlds, space travel, humanity's worth, or even what'll happen tomorrow. If I go by our history...we'll mess up again before long. But—" I blinked back tears. "I have never really needed to know the past or the future, judge who's worthy or not. I just play my part...make a happy home. When I'm not eating myself sick, getting jealous, or acting like a teenager on steroids."

Ben chuckled. "Yeah. About that. My fault. Okay, *our* fault." He shook his head. "I just needed to touch you, feel you close, and—" He lifted his hands in surrender.

"I understand." I swallowed. "I'm not done wanting you either. But loving means more than wanting. It means giving what's good and healthy, even when self-control isn't high on the priority list."

"So, how do we work this out?"

"Haven't a clue." I peered up into his eyes. "You're not Catholic by any chance?"

He smiled. "Try a Sacrament on me...I might like it."

I nestled my head on his chest. I could hear those somber voices singing in the blustery darkness, standing before the graves of those they loved, *I once was lost, but now I'm found...* We hadn't solved anything, exactly, but we had an understanding. And, for the moment, that would do.

Chapter Forty-Four

Naked in the Dark

Naked in the dark. That was me when I woke up stretched out on a strange hard bed. I couldn't see much; only a dim light illuminated the space around me—a steel-framed thing, cold to the touch. I lay flat on my back, the mattress thin but comfortable. The ceiling, a bland shade of off-white with no ornamentation, gave my mind nothing to consider, no hint of place or perspective.

I turned my head and tried to orientate myself, but dizziness swept over me.

Fear spread like poison through my mind.

Where am I?

Silence met my befuddled brain's frantic need to understand. Even as I clawed to consciousness, struggling to remember my name, my eyes closed, and darkness fell again.

~~~

A soft touch pressed my shoulder, dragging my brain back to the surface and fresh air. I opened my eyes.

A woman dressed in white with luminescent golden hair stood at my bedside, her fingers working over my shoulders, prodding as if to see that my bones were in the right place.

"Does that hurt?"

Groggy, I considered her words. *Hurt?* "No." Her touch felt warm and gentle, almost a caress. I flexed my fingers and felt along my sides. Naked flesh under
~~~

a light sheet. I swallowed and shook my head, rustling against the pillow's fabric.

She smiled down at me. "Good. It shouldn't, but with all you've been through, it's important to verify."

I fought to form words, like pushing a boulder up an incline. "Been...through?"

She nodded, her hands still busy turning and pressing unseen instruments.

A tube stretched from a distant point and looped over me...somewhere near my stomach. Horror ripped through me. "Where—am I?"

A slight tilt of the head and her clear blue eyes peered at me with serene calm and perhaps a tiny spark of curiosity. "At present, we are circling Earth, onboard the Triune's Ambassador."

I croaked my next words. "Why? I mean— Why am I here?" A chill raced over my arms as the next thought chased all other concerns away. "Juan, Dana—"

She patted my exposed shoulder. "They're fine. They have visited you several times. Good people." She pressed on my middle, her gaze fixed in studious concern.

A strange slithering sensation nearly pulled me upright as the tube retracted into the woman's hands. She grinned at me. "You're doing so well now; we won't need this anymore."

I fought back nausea. "What was that?"

Another tilt of the head as she pressed a bandage to my stomach. "You were suffering from anemia and a severely compromised immune system when we took you on board, so we had to feed you and perform necessary life-changing procedures. Soon you will be fully restored. Better than ever, in fact. The Triune has completed their interviews with Ben and your children and has been patiently awaiting *your* report."

I tried to sit up, needing a better view of not only

this strange woman but the room and my current life. “Report? I don’t know what you’re talking about. How long have I been here?”

The head of the bed rose without the accustomed motorized grind, lifting me into a sitting position.

She came from behind, and with a stronger grip than I expected, deftly stacked pillows at my sides to support me. “A month. It’s early February now, by your calendar. We had to treat your underlying disease and wait for your system to accept the change.” Her smile widened. “But you will feel like a new woman once you’ve finished your preparation.”

In combat for my emotions, terror fought with wild relief, as if someone taking complete control of my life was a welcome turn of events. “Preparation for what? Disease? I wasn’t sick...I would’ve noticed! Who the hell are you?” A thousand other questions spluttered on my lips.

She lifted her hand, a new look in her eyes. Sternness personified. “My name is Esrun, and I’ve been caring for you since you arrived. You were near death when we received you. If Ben hadn’t vouched for your character and your children hadn’t done so well in their interviews, we wouldn’t have bothered saving you. As it is now, you still have the finishing off process before your interview.” Her gaze locked onto mine. “If you would have any hope of salvation or a future for humanity, you had best cooperate. We won’t tolerate waste. We will make use of you one way or another. Either as an example of success—or failure. It is entirely up to you.”

Too surprised to respond, I merely gaped at her.

On to the business at hand, Esrun pointed across the room to what appeared to be a large bath or sauna. I couldn’t tell.

“Wash yourself and use whatever lotions appeal. There are a variety of soothing scents available. Clothing is in the cabinet. You may pick the style that fits your mood: dressy, casual, or what your daughter referred to as lumber-jack."

Stunned into default politeness, I stammered. "Th-thank you, Esrun."

"Relax. Meals will be provided at regular intervals. There is a sanctuary for your peace of mind beyond the door there, but you will have no visitors or distractions until your purification is complete. Once that is accomplished, you will be called for your interview."

I nodded despite haunting images of Juan and Dana rising in my mind. "Can't I see my children—know that they're all right?"

Esrun started for a door at the far end of the room. "Your children are fine, Rosie. They have already proven themselves. It's your turn now. You best make the most of your opportunity."

I threw my legs over the edge of the bed, defiantly testing my strength, which logically shouldn't exist after a month lying flat on my back. I stared at the retreating figure and watched her disappear out the door.

It shut with a definitive click.

I sucked in a deep breath.

Alone. No longer in the dark but as naked as ever.

Chapter Forty-Five

I Wasn't the Hero

I never realized how time had blurred by in my life until I spent time alone in tranquil beauty. After a long soak in the most comfortable bathtub I'd ever encountered, I babied my skin with lotions, smoothed and polished my nails, combed out my long hair, which remarkably seemed more chestnut brown than its former gray, and dressed in casual slacks, a comfy dark blue shirt, and a relaxed pair of sandals.

My body responded to luxury like an old family autocrat. Not eager to return to bed, I wandered out of my room to the sanctuary Esrun had pointed out.

Sanctuary indeed! This place rivaled fantasies of Heaven. Centered on a clear pond teeming with small fish, a prairie on one side and a wooded copse on the other, the whole thing seemed Eternal, a spot carved from natural perfection.

I started with the prairie. Wildflowers—Asters, Queen Anne's Lace, Bachelor Buttons, Black-eyed Susans, and Coneflowers stretched toward a bright light, not the sun, but just as enticing. I couldn't look directly up, as the blinding rays forbid even a peek, but the warmth and congenial lighting soothed every raw nerve in my body.

I wandered along a clear path, admiring the smallest details—colorful butterflies, energetic bees, a myriad of fluttering, buzzing, flying, and crawling critters. As a gentle breeze waved the grass and flowers, pleasant scents and sensations rippled through me. My heart slowed to the somnolent beat of a late summer day.

The green and blue pond glittered as the dangling fronds of an ancient weeping willow cascaded into the water like the tresses of a careless girl. Enchanted, I trod along the edge and fell under the spell of the matriarch of the woods, practically dancing beneath its foliage. I became a child again, playing hide and seek with fantasy and reality—present and past. Delighted, I immersed myself in the closest thing to joy that I had known since—when?

Ben.

Glorious sensations flooded me. His gentle touch. Lovemaking. Wholeness.

A chill swirled through, and my memory jumped to the next morning—his furrowed brow, my downcast gaze.

I hurried on.

The woods deepened, blocking the light, and shadows ruled. The path becoming confused.

Right or left?

A footstep ahead. I squinted.

Liam stood before me. His face exactly as it had been the moment when I kissed him at the airport—parting with quick reassurance—never to meet again. His melting eyes, so loving, so desperately in need of encouragement. *Did I ever love him...as he wanted me to?*

A sharp pain stabbed my chest. I reached out, stumbled, and fell, smacking my hands on the mossy ground.

A frightened chipmunk dived into a hole at the base of a tree.

Startled, I scrambled to my feet.

Nothing. No one.

Brushing the dirt off my hands, I wanted to smile, but my lips trembled. *I'm sorry, Liam. I did love you. As best I could. I don't know if it was enough.*

A sob choked my throat.

"Mom!" Dana's voice.

I glanced around for her imperious figure, her appraising gaze. The quiet hum of insects droned on without interruption.

Dana would sneer at my histrionics.

Dana—my darling baby girl. The one I almost lost. After losing the twins...I shoved fresh pain away. *I got over that—a long time ago. Wasn't meant to be.*

Clenching my jaw, I marched through the darkened woods, slapping prickly vines out of my way, disturbed by the darkness that made everything menacing. *It can't be nightfall...can it?*

My heart raced as I pounded forward, frantic to get back to the prairie and the open light.

A branch hit me in the face. Thwap!

A new memory came to life before my eyes. I had just turned fourteen when the pretty senior, Maxine, knocked into me. My school books crashed to the floor.

She stood there, one hand on her curvaceous hip, her eyes wide with surprise, completely unaware of the pain she was causing. "Didn't see you, kid. You're invisible, know that?"

I knew. Frozen by the vividness of the image, I squeezed my eyes shut and waited for the rising terror to subside. *This isn't real. It can't be.*

A murder of crows broke from the treetops and screeched, cawing, into the sky. Blinking my eyes open, I searched my environment.

Still. Quiet. Alone.

The insects had quieted. Maxine was gone, as was Liam and the twins. I inched my way forward, reaching out to avoid any low-hanging branches or looping vines. Dread churned my stomach.

Darkness continued to descend.

Stepping carefully didn't protect me. In that journey through the thicket, I relived some of the most trying episodes of my life.

The time I told my sister Sarah that I wish she were dead—and meant it—over a stupid game gone wrong.

Early dating episodes with Rog and his fast fingers.

Mom's memory lapses that I ignored for too long.

Dad's impending heart attack and my denial until they couldn't revive him in the emergency room.

The graveside burial for twin babies born much too early.

Liam's absences, his ridiculous obsessions, and irritating childishness while I craved another baby of my own.

Dana's unpredictable temper.

The adoption process and Juan's birthmother's desperation.

Never-ending housework.

Body aches and rounds of the flu.

Rising with the sun and dropping onto my bed, exhausted.

Depression. Guilt. Loneliness.

Maddened like a tormented bull, I broke through the final line of trees and entered the prairie at twilight. Moonlight—or so it seemed—filtered from above.

I stopped on the edge of the pond as a soft glow glimmered in ever-expanding circles, and I sobbed my heart out.

For what?

For myself, as a child hurt by a thousand misunderstandings, cruelties, and blind dead ends.

For countless stupidities and selfish acts that I perpetuated on others, which I should never have meant but did.

For disillusioned innocence, the tearing wrench of death, the sting of guilt, the hopelessness of ignorance, and the chastisement of looking over my shoulder and knowing that I could have made better choices.

The searing pain when others did me wrong carelessly and intentionally. And I returned the evil favor.

I wasn't the hero of my own story.

~~~

Esrun woke me with a gentle nudge. "Time for your interview, Rosie."

I sat up, rubbing my eyes like a child after a long slumber. *What? Where?*

Oh, yeah.... My blinding, choking, no-holds-barred cry at the edge of the pond in the glimmering moonlight filled my coming-to-consciousness mind. Then I relaxed in the calm peace which had enveloped me as I padded back to my room.

I looked at the tub where I'd had taken a long soak and then rubbed my soft pajamas, found conveniently on the counter by the sink.

As I looked up, Esrun held out the dressy outfit—a silky blue top over loose white pantaloons and embroidered slippers.

Without comment, I accepted the bundle and trod off to the bathroom. I accomplished my morning ablutions, making every effort to rinse the redness out of my puffy eyes, and prepared myself for the meeting of a lifetime.

Me against the Triune. Face to face. A lowly human answering to universal forces. I swallowed back bile. There was no way this could turn out well.

Sucking in a deep, cleansing breath, I paced back into the main room and stopped before Esrun. "If Ben, Dana, and Juan did well, then I have a chance of surviving, eh?"

Esrun tilted her head in that particular way she had, as if considering an unusual viral symptom. "To those much is given, much is expected." With that, she turned and led the way to a distant, unfamiliar doorway. One I was terrified to pass through.

God, help me.
~~~

Chapter Forty-Six

Is This What You Really Want?

The greatest antidote to intimidation was humility. It wasn't that I felt strong, brave, smart, or particularly good, but I knew—to the depth of my being—that I wasn't as strong as I had hoped, as brave as I'd dreamed, as smart as I'd believed, or as good as I needed to be. Not exactly the *wretch* of *Amazing Grace*, but pretty darn close. I trod along the white curving corridor, a dead woman walking. Judged and found guilty by my own standards, I knew there wasn't much hope. I and the whole human race had failed momentously.

Strangely, it no longer felt like such a big deal.

Anticlimactic confirmation teemed through my being.

Not for one moment was I God or goodness incarnate. *Should've realized that long ago...*

Esrun stopped at a foyer and waved toward a white, nondescript door. "Your guardian will take you from here." With a smile, she patted my arm and met my gaze. "It was a privilege to serve you, Rosie."

Astonished, I batted back tears. *Don't do that, woman. Alien. Whatever you are. Right now, kindness might just kill me.*

A tall, imposing figure stepped forward—a man's-man by every definition. Dark golden hair, sky blue eyes, muscled build, a gentle smile, and a courtly wave announced his readiness for a starring role in whatever was coming next.

Only he didn't seem to know that.

Without offering a name or position, he simply led me into a small, enclosed space, an elevator of sorts, with a large window facing the starry universe. We rose, a hardly noticeable event according to the view, but my stomach insisted that we were moving upward.

A door slid open, and we paced into a huge space at least two hundred meters long with an ornate domed ceiling. Something between a Cathedral and a museum dazzled my eyes.

A golden tower at the end of the room glinted in the muted light. Along the walls, antiquities from human history stood on pedestals and adorned wall niches. Sections of ancient cave paintings hung from fixed poles, pottery, early manuscripts, tapestries, weapons of all kinds—spears, battle-axes, bows and arrows, longbows, guns, and tasers—lined sturdy, see-through shelves.

I turned around, trying to take it all in—my breath catching in my throat. Mounted animals and birds filled an entire section, a progression of advancement that overwhelmed my mind.

I glanced at my guide.

His gaze stayed fixed on the tower at the far end.

"Excuse me, but could you tell—"

Three figures paced from the far end toward me.

With only a nod and a slight smile, my guide backed away. One flicked hand motion directed me to focus on who was coming.

I took the hint.

The three men stopped before me. One was an elderly figure in a long white robe, the next was a middle-aged man wearing a short gray tunic, the third appeared to be in his prime—dressed like a common man of my era in jeans and a dark blue shirt. They exuded calm, but their penetrating gazes denoted thoughtful intensity.

An unspoken command to bow or kneel—show some formal respect—pounded against my brain. But despite my newfound humility, I could not act on the command. I would not. Not unless my conscience understood and agreed. *Stubborn as ever.*

The elderly figure took a step forward, one hand pressed on his chest. "I am Rehtaf. Here are my brothers, Nos and Tirips. We are glad to finally meet you in person, Rosie."

To my utter discomfort, my body trembled, and my voice shook when I answered, "I can't say I am glad, but I'll be grateful to finally understand what's been happening—to myself—to the whole human race." In the most audacious leap of my life, I glared at them and asked, "Who on Earth are you?"

Not on Earth, obviously. I held my ground. The question still stood.

Rehtaf shook his head, smiling. "I thought you knew. You once said that that *we* were obvious."

Nos pointed to a distant cluster of furniture. "Let's sit and be comfortable as we discuss matters, shall we?"

I followed like a schoolchild, wishing I could escape for the holiday. There was a lesson coming that I didn't want to learn. *Could anything be worse than last night's crash course in humility?*

In a cozy alcove, the three settled on a plush green couch amid a riot of flowing plants.

I perched on the edge of a straight-backed chair. I needed to keep my feet on the floor.

Rehtaf waved at my guardian, who, to my surprise, had followed along and stood waiting. "Refreshments, please."

Without further instruction, the guardian paced away.

Nos eyed me, delving into my soul. "Who do you think we are, Rosie?"

I hated exams, especially if my life was on the line. Pass and I return to Earth. Fail, and I descend into the fires of Hell, maybe?

With a shudder, I glanced up—*Save me!*—and told the truth. "Rehtaf is father spelled backward. Nos is son. And Tirips is spirit. So, you are either God in three alien forms or you are imitators—for good or evil—I can't say exactly. Though from what I've seen—you've caused the death of millions—you can't be the God I've believed in all my life. You must be devils."

A shared look among the three left me nearly hyperventilating.

Nos spoke up first. "You are perceptive, Rosie. We assumed as much. With your DNA, you certainly should be. But you are also wrong."

To my utter consternation, he chuckled.

Heat rose in my face. "What are you saying? Stop being so damn clever and just tell me the truth!"

Tirips lifted his hand, a gesture of conciliation and command. "You are family, Rosie. Your DNA matches very closely with ours. We are not gods but merely created beings like yourself. Many humans carry selections of our DNA, some more than others, so we are family—as fathers, sons, and even in spirit—we are your kin."

Baffled, I slapped my hands to my face and tried to rub the memory of yesterday's tears into oblivion. "So why have you tortured us? Caused the human race so much pain and suffering?"

A perplexed expression filled Rehtaf's face. "We only did as you begged us to. As technology took root in your society, self-destruction loomed ever nearer. You perfected your weapons, grew addicted to feedback loops and embedded identity chips, allowed unfeeling bots to rule integral systems, lost your collective sense of humanity in a morass of self-obsession and isolation, became dependent on chemical enhancements, and denied your need for family and cultural identity. You faced extinction at your own hands. We simply slowed the process, to give a remnant of humanity a chance to decide—is this what you really want?"

Stunned, I lost the power of linear thought, much

less coherent speech. *We asked for this?* And like a child facing the rule of discipline, actions, and consequences, I knew it was true.

Nos pressed my shoulder with a kindly touch. "We do not hate the human race, Rosie. We love you as our own, but we refused your poison long ago. Our people have been emigrating to new planets for centuries, and Earth is among the choicest offerings. We hoped for better things from you."

My vision cleared, and I understood. Humanity was not alone, and we did not have an exclusive right to the planet or even to our own race. We were a part of something so much greater—something we had never dared to dream. I locked onto Tirips—as he seemed more familiar. "You are one of us, really?"

Guardian approached with a tray of steaming mugs and biscuit-thingies.

Tirips rose and accepted the tray. He laid it on an end table next to the couch and passed the drinks. He swung his gaze from me to my guardian. "Like Ben—he was left on this planet years ago and grew old there. He was one of the first we contacted when we returned. We sent Ben to you."

Clutching the warm cup in my hands, I shook my head at embarrassing memories.

Tirips sipped his drink, stared at me, and then sighed.

Heat flushed my face once again. I imagined a red balloon ready to burst.

Nos bent forward, laying a hand on my knee. "You are no longer broken, at least not completely. You will heal. Beyond allowing you to face your greatest weaknesses and overcome your worst self, we also adjusted your cells so that they are as they were meant to be. Those with enough of our DNA have the ability to live much longer than the average human. Even humans with the weaker DNA could live much longer, if given the right treatment—but there is no use assisting people if they have no desire to survive."

Nearly gasping from shock, I had to force out my next words. "You fixed my DNA? So, how long can I live now?"

"Another hundred years or so. You and Ben can live your final days together."

The Guardian stepped closer, followed by three familiar figures: Ben, Juan, and Dana.

My heart lurched in joy.

Ben smiled. Dana waved. Juan offered a peace sign.

I dragged my gaze back to the three alien men. "And the human race, our technology? Can we have it back?"

They spoke as one. "Only if you can handle it."

Looking from my children, to Ben, then to the three people who were not my enemies, I opened my heart to what I so desperately needed—faith, hope, and love.

Chapter Forty-Seven

We Have Yet to Become

Eight Years Later

It was a beautiful spring afternoon. The cherry, apple, and pear trees were in bloom. Strawberries were ripe for the picking on the hill. Robins and woodpeckers scavenged for early bugs and worms. Fluffy white clouds sailed across an azure sky.

My husband, Ben, and my son-in-law, David—Dana's husband—planted the vegetable garden with the tomato, pepper, and zucchini seedlings that I had started in late February. The onions and potatoes were already up, greening one side of the field. Juan and his wife worked the other side of the garden, setting plants in place and arranging the herbs in a decorative order. Dana minded the babies while watching her eldest daughter, Sophia, swing on the jungle rope over the creek bed.

I pulled my gaze from the window back to the sink, thrilled once again at the feeling of hot water rushing over my sticky fingers. The process of making bread had not changed, but the cleanup was so much easier now that we had simple amenities like running water, washing machines, and electric lights.

Thank you, God.

A constant prayer, like breathing, I lived an attitude of gratitude even when hardship happened. Yesterday, we had attended the funeral of Delmar Bolder, grieving alongside his widow, one of the strongest women I ever knew. Patty wasn't a spring chicken, but she had the gumption of ten women and had already taken in two other widows with their combined five kids and two grandchildren. Her strength and goodness would bear witness to another generation, and Delmar, in death as well as life, would support her.

I'll drop by those extra tomato seedlings tomorrow. Bet she could use some of David's honey too. Wonder if she'd share that recipe for—

A screech yanked my attention to the kitchen porch. Banging and yelling foretold an epic battle.

I hurried forward and jerked open the screen door.

Dana practically tumbled into the room, holding two squirming babies, one in each arm.

Seven-year-old Sophia pranced into the room like a princess going on stage. "They're stinky, Gram! Mom says they timed it just right—two for one."

I grabbed Juan's wiggling son, baby Liam, while Dana wrestled with her youngest, who I smirkingly referred to as Dana's Inferno.

"Lord, Mom, you prayed for this, didn't you? A little girl with the personality of a tornado."

Baby Liam gurgled and wiggled in my arms, a strong aroma assaulting my nose. *Oh, yeah. He needs a change all right.* I patted Dana's shoulder as I headed for the bathroom. "God has a way of evening the score when we least expect it."

When the little ones were cleaned up and playing happily with pots and pans on the kitchen floor, I returned to my bread-making.

Dana put a few more sticks into the woodstove while Sophia drew a picture on the kitchen table. I glanced at her newest artistic creation, impressed by the child's innate ability. "I'll never get beyond stick people, even if I do live another hundred years or so."

Dana chuckled. "She didn't get it from me. Must be a throwback. Or maybe David's been hiding secret abilities." She wiggled her eyebrows and grinned. "He's always surprising me, that man."

I plunked the last of the dough into a bread pan and shoved the four loaves into the oven. Washing my fingers in the wonderfully warm water, I spoke over my shoulder. “So, you don’t miss the big city life and all that you planned to do when you left home the first time?”

Dana swiped drool off her baby’s chin, shaking her head. “I still do the work I love, just with more family in my day than I originally planned.” She tossed a towel over her shoulder, leaned on the counter, and eyed me. “Are you happy, Mom? The way things worked out—no retirement in your future. No trips to exotic locations and days to do as you please. You may live longer, but life is a lot harder this way.”

On impulse, I trotted to the living room, swiped a leather-bound volume off a high shelf, and returned with it tucked under my arm. Sucking in a bracing intake of air, I handed it over.

Perplexed, Dana accepted it with two hands. “But this is yours. You’ve been working on it for years.”

My smile wasn’t a happy one. More a message of contentment than joy. “We made a deal—you, me, Ben, Juan, and your spouses. We chose an intentional way of life. It’s not for everyone. There are those who will still strive for the greatest and latest in technology and innovation. But here”—I tapped the book—“is the reason why we live as we do.”

Dana pulled out a chair and slid the book onto the table.

Sophia scowled at the invasion of her drawing space.

I stepped up and flipped the book open, my unruly script trailing across the pages. I turned to the middle section and a blank page. “It’s time you started helping me write this.”

Dana tilted her head, resting it on an arm propped on the table, weariness oozing from her eyes. “I spend my day working online, helping Dave, and taking care of my miniature terrors. I don’t have time to journal.”

Sophia’s scowl deepened; her crayon scraped hard

on the paper as she ran a purple color in wide circles around the figures in the middle. "This is the world, mama. You better not break it, or we'll all leak into space!"

I plunked down and took Dana's hands in my own. "Daughter of mine, I love you more than my own heart, but you cannot shirk this duty. I don't record our lives to simply inform the next generation of our daily do, I leave a record of humanity's failures and successes. I trust that the Sophia's and all the babies yet to come will read it, learn from it, and grow beyond it."

With a loud sigh, Dana pulled back her hands and flipped through the pages. "People will still screw up, Mom. Look at what happened on the east coast. That engineered DNA replicator was a disaster."

With a deep sigh, I rose from the table and started setting the table for dinner to the tune of boots clumping up the porch steps. "I know, honey. This isn't a promise of salvation for the human race as we know it. It's hope for a human race we have yet to become."

Chapter Forty-Eight

Home

I sat on a blanket with Ben at my side, the kids and grandkids playing around an evening fire, red and orange embers spiraling upward to a star-studded sky. Even my sister Sarah, her husband Bill, and their little boy, Caleb, had come for a summer visit. Despite my joy, I shivered as night's chill descended.

Ben wrapped his arm around me and pulled me close.

I rested my head on his shoulder, relaxing in the end-of-a-busy-day weariness.

He tilted his head back and pointed. "They're coming. In the not-so-distant future, others will arrive. But this time, the aliens won't plant seeds. They'll come to claim the harvest."

Protective determination rushing through me, I lay back and waved away his dire predictions. "Let them come. We are not helpless or hopeless anymore. Humanity has a future. Here and even"—I pointed—"out there."

Ben relaxed and lay back, folding one arm behind his head. He sighed. In contentment or resignation, I could not say.

Sophia shrieked.

I lifted my head and glanced about the backlit night scene.

Sarah, Bill, and little Caleb watched, grinning.

David scooped his wild little girl into his arms.

Dana stood next to the picnic table and rocked her baby boy, singing in a glorious voice I never knew she had:

Rock-a-bye baby

On the treetops,

When the wind blows

The cradle will rock.

When the bough breaks...

Moving in gently, Juan wrapped his arms around his wife, Carrie, who cuddled their son in her arms, an image of fruitful family love if ever there was one.

When the bough breaks.... I returned my gaze to the stars above, reaching for Ben's hand. "We can't ever fail again...can we?"

Ben clasped my hand and held it tight. "There's the rub. Some people will fail. Instead of transformation, they'll descend into wild beasts. But that's not what the Triune meant. They warned that if we, as a race of beings, don't value our role as stewards, others will come and be given our inheritance."

Extinction? Shivers ran down my arms. Tears filled my eyes at the thought of Sophia being the last of her kind.

The little girl wiggled free of her father's arms and ran pell-mell around the yard, shrieking as loud as ever.

Dana smirked, adjusting her baby on her hip. "Whoa, David, get on your game, or our seven-year-old will outrun you!"

Juan jumped to his brother-in-law's rescue and ran interference, trying to block the child's darting maneuvers.

Carrie beamed, settling her son on his feet and waving his hands, tempting her niece. "Hey, Sophia, someone wants you!"

Like a bee drawn to honey, the girl ran to the baby and hugged him.

Coming to a sudden halt and heaving deep breaths, David and Juan clapped each other on the back and shared an eye-roll.

The rest of the family burst out laughing.

Ben sat up, tugging my arm. “Come on, woman, David and Juan will take care of the sheep, but we have to check on the cows, make sure the chickens are in for the night and get ready for an early start tomorrow. That broken fence won’t mend itself.”

With a barely noticeable groan, I rose and grabbed Ben’s supportive arm. “At this rate, I’m not sure how I’ll make it through another ninety-two years. Or thereabout.” I considered the kids, and sadness enveloped me. “How come only us—and no one else?”

“Ben clutched my hand and led me forward. “Because *we* are the last of our kind, my love.”

~~~

Early the next morning, I stepped out onto my bedroom porch and soaked in the warm, brilliant blue-sky sunshine. Sparrows, robins, blue jays, and a couple of cardinals fluttered about in springtime joy.

Home.

There was no place else I’d rather be.
~~~

About the Author

Mother, Educator, Writer, Manager,
and Captain of my ship

As a teacher with a degree in Elementary Education who has taught in big cities and small towns, Ann Frailey homeschooled all of her children. She manages her rural homestead with her kids and their numerous critters. She writes books and a Friday blog alternating between short stories and her My Road Goes Ever On series.

Her nonfiction work focuses on the intersection of motherhood, widowhood, practicing gratitude, and rediscovering joy.

Her fiction novels expand from the OldEarth world to the Newearth universe—where deception rules but truth prevails.

She earned a Masters of Fine Arts Degree in Creative Writing for Entertainment from Full Sail University.

In her spare time, she serves as an election judge and as secretary/treasurer of her small town's cemetery.

She is currently finishing a new science fiction novel in the Newearth world and a historical fiction & science fiction blend in her OldEarth series. To check out her stories, novels, inspirational books, and her film and tv scripts, visit https://akfrailey.com/

www.ingramcontent.com/pod-product-compliance
Lightning Source LLC
Chambersburg PA
CBHW070615310726
48982CB00001B/93
9781732395275